The Bad-News Man

The Bad-News Man

MARY McMULLEN

PUBLISHED FOR THE CRIME CLUB BY
DOUBLEDAY & COMPANY, INC.
GARDEN CITY, NEW YORK
1986

All of the characters in this book
are fictitious, and any resemblance
to actual persons, living or dead,
is purely coincidental.

Library of Congress Cataloging-in-Publication Data
McMullen, Mary, 1920–
The bad-news man.
I. Title.
PS3563.A31898B33 1986   813'.54   85–46076
ISBN 0-385-23435-X

To Dru, Kim and Jason

The Bad-News Man

ONE

"There's a leak in the roof, right by the chimney, in the east cottage," Maria Captiva reported with her usual relish when toting up the day's problems. "The laundry'll be two or three hours late, the van broke down near Race Point. Major Yardley's bathroom sink is stopped up, and he says he's tried the plunger and it doesn't work. Ma says cranberry juice has just gone up ten cents a quart."

As usual, she was a little disappointed when Mrs. Lockett, seated at her desk in her small office off the entrance sitting room, looked her composed pink and white self on hearing these announcements.

"There's backup laundry in my linen closet across the street. I'll see to the other things, except I can't do much about the price of cranberry juice," Mrs. Lockett said serenely. "And a little problem for you, Maria, the Waynes left early for Boston, and Mrs. Wayne put her head in here and said the little boy had done crayon drawings all over the bathroom wall. I don't think they'd be much good to us as murals, so use whatever's best when it comes to scrubbing the bathroom."

It was nine o'clock on a fine sunny June morning after the night's heavy rain. Mrs. Lockett had risen at seven and had her tea and toast in her apartment in the house across the street from the inn, which she still thought of as Miss Winthrop's house but was now hers.

She had dallied briefly with the idea of moving out of her upstairs rooms into the large downstairs quarters occupied by Miss Winthrop for thirty-odd years, but had decided she was entirely comfortable with her own arrangements. Why not turn the downstairs into a deluxe sort of suite to be rented out, big bedroom, big kitchen, large bath, living room looking into a little grove of willows with a goldfish pond at their feet. She was sure there would be takers for it, even at upped prices; the Lilacs had few empty rooms for more than a day or so at a stretch, from the Fourth of July until well after Labor Day.

And besides, the memories . . . even though she didn't think of herself as a fanciful, sentimental woman. The broad bed with the shell-carved mahogany headboard, where Anne had peacefully died in her sleep at the age of seventy-eight almost four months ago. The long chair covered in rose-colored silk, by the window, where Anne stretched out at leisure hours reading her books. The photographs of her mother and father, her dead brother, her friends, in silver frames on the chest of drawers. And the presence there, which seemed to remain for some time afterwards, autocratic, individual, the sound of a quietly commanding voice, the faint sharp scent of the Spanish lavender toilet water she always used.

At the end of May, refurbishing the downstairs rooms had been completed, fresh paint and wallpaper, a new jade green broadloom rug replacing the all-but-priceless old Oushak in the living room, everything of Anne Winthrop's neatly packed away in boxes and placed reverentially in the attic. Everything except the photographs, which in her will she had stipulated be sent to her only near relative, a niece living in Florence, her brother Edward's only child.

Occasionally, over the years, Miss Winthrop had mused aloud on the disposition of her property after her death. Not in any mood of melancholy, or advice-seeking, but merely considering possibilities. Arabella, her niece, had married an Italian of great wealth. "Besides, I never liked the girl, she takes after her mother. Girl indeed! Late fifties by now, and from her Christmas letters I gather has made a hobby of being an invalid, or really I think the other way round."

Another year, she had considered leaving it to her college, Wellesley, as a vacation home for members of the teaching staff. And then, as she was a habitual reader, going from Dickens and Trollope, Jane Austen and Thackeray, to her other literary loves, detective novels, she thought an end-of-the-town extension of the public library would be a pleasant use for the Lilacs.

Once when she had pneumonia at the age of sixty-nine, and was rather worried about her survival, she said to Mrs. Lockett, "Whatever happens, your home here will be secured always." By which Mrs. Lockett took it to mean that her rooms would be left to her rent-free, for her lifetime.

On that first bewildered, numbed, grieving day in March after Miss Winthrop's death in her sleep, she had found herself thinking, That's all very well, but what if the heirs decide to sell? Then where am I? She had a savings account of her own, and in not too far-distant a time would get Social Security, but her wonderings, which made her feel deeply guilty, were not about straitened means: the Lilacs was her life.

These thoughts were brought on by a gloomy forecast from Major Yardley, who had been for eight years a year-round tenant in the Lilacs' west cottage.

Standing looking out at the rain sweeping in veils across Cape Cod Bay, he had said, "Of course, the place will be sold out from under us, and they'll build condominiums or some other horrible thing here. It's a very choice site."

The day after the funeral was the worst of all. Sad as that occasion was, sad and final, there had been a bustle of people and things to be seen to. A great many people:

Miss Winthrop while not being a popular favorite was widely known and well respected in Provincetown. And people from New York, from Boston, from Wellesley, many of whom had been summertime regulars at the Lilacs. The Episcopal church of St. Mary's of the Harbor was filled almost to capacity.

Everything was done properly, in Miss Winthrop's style, a splendid buffet, a generously stocked liquors table, in the big breakfast room at the inn, people overflowing into the sitting room. The at least temporary cheer of old friends reuniting, a babble of talk, and, yes, here and there laughter. People couldn't help that, it was a form of survival.

Then, the next day, the crash of silence, all but unbearable. The loss, the end of things, real and sharp as steel.

At two o'clock in the afternoon, Miss Winthrop's lawyer, John Boxx, made vigorous use of the door knocker. He said he was very sorry that he hadn't been able to attend the funeral as he had been in White Sulphur Springs visiting an aunt who was very ill and on the point of death herself.

Then he got out a heavy envelope from the breast pocket of his topcoat and before referring to its contents in detail told Mrs. Lockett that she was Miss Winthrop's heir. The entire estate left to her outright, except for some photographs to be sent to her niece in Florence.

Even now, she was sometimes surprised awake at night by a dream that it *was* a dream—wasn't it? No. Astonishing as it was, it was real, it was true.

Sitting at her desk, the clap of joy came over her again, in broad daylight. Finger in her address book, about to look up the plumber's telephone number, she gazed across the bay without seeing it, the blue of it, the morning glisten, the windsurfer near the little beach toppling off his craft and getting back on.

It's mine. The inn, the dwelling house, the two cottages, the land, the furniture, the garden, the towering lilac hedge along the road, all of this is mine.

Well, go ahead and look up the number, but take another minute to savor this feeling, that she was the luckiest and happiest woman in the world.

She was just dialing when Major Yardley entered the office carrying a large bouquet of Queen Anne's lace, wild flax, and pink-lavender vetch. He stood listening while she requested firmly that immediate attention be paid to the stopped-up sink in the west cottage at the Lilacs. "Oh, good, in under an hour you say? While you're here, you might check the toilet in the lavatory off the inn kitchen, I think the chain in the tank may be loose or even broken, perhaps it should be replaced."

Hanging up, she smiled at her visitor. "Well, you did catch me at just the right moment, taking care of your sink." He was a tall man in his late fifties, militarily lean and erect, his face thin, his eyes bright blue, his small mustache and gingery-gray hair trimmed in a no-nonsense way.

Major Yardley hesitated. To go from toilet tanks to flowers required something of a verbal bridge. And this was an entirely new gesture on his part, the bouquet in his hand. He hadn't the vocabulary yet for these things.

(He had wanted to gather some of the inn garden flowers, not much caring for what he termed weeds, in his hand, but he thought that that would hardly do.)

"Fine morning," he said. "I've just had my walk." This hardly constituted news as almost every morning of the year he stalked smartly to the Town Hall and back, a round trip of about three miles. Forgetting for a moment his floral offering, he went on, "The usual trash jamming the center of town, have to pick your way through these fellows. Gets worse every year. I saw a man or I think it was a man in a woman's cocktail-party sort of dress with makeup on his face and shiny things—sequins?—pasted onto his eyebrows. Revolting." Even after eight years, the Provincetown summer influx had not lost its power to shock him; he was perpetually indignant and vocally appalled throughout this surging season.

He objected violently to the term "gay." "What's gay about them? What've they got to be gay about? Misfits, all out of step, the whole bunch. Why, *my mother's name was Gay!*"

Mrs. Lockett made a sympathetic, murmuring noise of mild agreement, and then he held out his bouquet. "Picked these for you along the way, thought they might brighten up your desk." He had intended to be casual about it, but he flushed a strong red.

Well, what next, thought Mrs. Lockett. "How nice, aren't they pretty. Thank you. I'll go get a vase."

He looked relieved to beat his own hasty retreat as she got up and left her office, carrying the wildflowers. She went through the dining room, where ten or so people were breakfasting. The Lilacs was now, in the last week of June, less than half full. Casting an inspecting eye here and there—yes, there were fresh marguerites from the garden on each occupied table—and scattering cheerful good-mornings, she went into the big kitchen.

Breakfast was the only meal served. Maria Captiva waited on the tables and in between helped her mother Angela with the cooking. When the guest rooms began to fill up, Mrs. Lockett would pitch in and help, scrambling eggs, frying bacon, pouring cranberry or orange juice, sliding in pans of blueberry muffins to bake.

From a shelf in the butler's pantry, she took a homely green pottery pitcher for her flowers. She was still a little puzzled at the major's offering, and his suddenly red face. Was it just a gentlemanly celebration of a fine sunny morning, or . . . ?

Years ago, Miss Winthrop had said to her, "I wonder you don't marry again. Not that I'd like losing you, in fact I rather think you are irreplaceable. But, seeing you from a man's point of view, you're a cozy, homey body. Even-tempered, a good cook, and you're really quite nice to look upon." Mrs. Lockett had replied that she was happy the way she was and intended to remain that way.

Marry again?

Once had been enough. Once had been more than enough.

TWO

Mondays and Thursdays were the days when Mrs. Lockett did her professional and private shopping. Any other errands to be done were scheduled for the same trips.

Before she left, at eleven o'clock, she had the regrettable but pleasant task of taking three long-distance phone calls and politely refusing reservations for the long weekend of the Fourth of July, the Fourth falling this year on a Tuesday. "I'm very sorry, we're booked solid." It was nice to think of the Lilacs humming along at full capacity.

She rechecked her grocery list, saw that she had left out the flounder, which Major Yardley liked broiled for his breakfast on Sundays, and added it. Special orders were not taken from regular guests, but as a year-rounder the major was an exception.

Let's see, library books to be returned, piled up on the table near the door in the sitting room. She paused for an automatic checkup in the mirror over the table. Neat, clean, tidy, all well with her appearance.

She was a woman of medium height, fifty-eight years of age, gently inclined to plumpness. She wore no makeup, her pink-flushed fair skin being of a naturally powdery matte finish. Her eyes were the clear light blue of the wild flax in the major's bouquet. Her hair was gray, permanently waved, and knotted at the nape. She wore today a dress very much like all her other dresses, small-flowered, belted at the waist, of permanent-press cotton and polyester, so easy to keep nice and fresh. She had never cared for pantyhose and wore instead nylon stockings, which were increasingly hard to come by, held up by the garters of her firm girdle. She had never been seen bare-legged except for the occasional dip in the bay. Her sandals were of beige leather, comfortable, with medium heels.

Going out, she looked up at the low gray sky and thought she caught a smell of rain in the air. When she crossed Commercial Street to get her car out of the garage behind the house, she stopped to get her umbrella from the hall closet.

Groceries the main job, take care of that first. Cudworth's Grocery was on Bradford and close to the center of town. She parked her car in Cudworth's lot and spent twenty or so minutes, neither hurrying nor dawdling, making her purchases.

Long ago, Miss Winthrop had struck a bargain with Cudworth's. All the Lilacs' supplies to be bought there, right down to soap powder and toilet tissue, and then when the bill for each order was added up, twenty per cent to be taken off the total. The store would deliver her order, and Mrs. Lockett could have done it all over the telephone, but she liked to assure with her own eye that the oranges for the fresh juice were in prime condition, the bacon lean, the blueberries ripe and plump.

She left her car in the store lot because parking places along Commercial Street, where she was now heading, were not easy to find. She went to the post office for a book of stamps, then to the library where she browsed for a while and then settled on several light romances by a writer she found trustworthy in this department—no indecencies jumping up off the page at you, no crude business about people's bodies, except the strong loving arms and the allowably passionate kiss.

Coming out of the library, she saw the stream of people pouring off MacMillan Wharf, a familiar noontime manifestation. The excursion boat from Boston arrived daily, its passengers viewed in several different lights. Often when Miss Winthrop's eye had lit on the invaders, she had said mildly, "Vulgus odio," and let it go at that. Those in the business of selling hot dogs, hamburgers and beer welcomed the large consumption of these items. The better restaurants and shops expected little or no custom from this crowd, but novelty stores prospered, and there were even dealings in the world of art: scenes of dunes, breaking waves, lighthouses and rose-covered cottages, proclaimed as "hand-painted oil paintings," bought and proudly carried back to the boat when it left the wharf to return to Commonwealth Pier in Boston at three-thirty.

"Tacky-looking bunch, but at least they're not all queer," was Major Yardley's general reaction.

With the skill of long practice, Mrs. Lockett made her way along the crowded sidewalk, stepping off into the street when necessary, and then back onto the sidewalk again. She was a few doors away from the Mayflower Cafe, where she thought she might drop in and have one of their delicious and moderately priced lobster rolls, when she saw him.

Standing at an open-fronted hotdog stand, one of a dozen or so customers.

Maybe it was someone who just looked like him.

She hadn't, after all, seen him for twenty-six years.

Then she heard his voice, saying to the pretty girl behind the counter, "Grill me another, dear, and I'll have a glass of that orange-colored chemical stuff to wash it down with."

His back was to her. She passed perhaps four feet from him, and not daring to look behind her to see if he had for some reason turned his head, crossed to the other side of the street with seven or eight people when the light turned red.

Crossing again at the far side of Town Hall, she turned off Commercial into Ryder Street and began to walk very fast toward Bradford.

She had almost gotten to Cudworth's parking lot when the near-faintness swept her, the earth took an unexpected turn on its axis, and she found herself grasping a picket fence in front of a neat little lawn. Just wait a minute or so, just breathe deeply. Yes, turn your head now, you have to, even if . . .

There weren't many people on Ryder Street. And he was not one of them.

Would her legs work? They did. She unlocked her car, got in, and drove away.

The Lilacs had never looked to her more safe, more welcoming. Serenely changeless in a world boiling with change. In fact, it had looked very much as it had, all those years ago, when she had first arrived, as a guest, as a fugitive.

She was twenty-nine when she married Cosmo Fane; or rather, when he married her.

They had met at a cocktail party given by a friend of hers after the two young women attended a concert at Carnegie Hall. One of the guests, proudly presented by her friend Louise, had been playing with the orchestra that afternoon. He was a cellist.

He was also tall, with a dramatic sweep of dark hair dipping over his forehead, warm flashing large dark eyes, an imposing nose and a charming slow smile.

She was a well-paid and efficient executive secretary to the vice-president of a Wall Street brokerage firm. She had a rosy, dimply charm of her own, was a little plump, and was a delightfully good listener, especially to a man who played his cello at Carnegie Hall on a snowy January afternoon.

In a corner, after he had brought her her second drink, he told her a little about himself. He was, he said, composing a symphony and earning his bread meanwhile by playing with various orchestras; he also played the piano. "Fill-in work here, there, and everywhere, when some orchestra member gets sick or doesn't choose to turn up for rehearsals," he said with pleasing modesty. "But a regular position wouldn't give me time for my own work, so I go hither and thither, New York, Wilmington, Philadelphia, Boston, Chicago."

There was in his voice a slight tinge of somewhere-in-Europe accent, which gave to the most pedestrian statement a quality of mystery and romance.

Louise, who had no intention of leaving her distinguished guest solely to the company of May Morris, interrupted the promising téte-a-téte to introduce him to a nearby group.

But the next morning, a dozen long-stemmed white roses were delivered to May's apartment, with a note, "Shall I be bold enough to hope to see you tonight, without seventeen other people to get in the way of our acquaintance? Louise was kind enough to give me the name of the firm where you work. I will call you this afternoon if I may . . . *May.* Yours, Cosmo Fane."

"Well! After you left he buttonholed me," Louise reported over the phone before lunchtime, her voice half peevish and half intrigued, "wanting to know everything about you. Where you worked, what you did, were you married or seriously involved, what your home address was, everything. Naturally, I told him you had lots of men around but as far as I knew hadn't made up your mind about any particular one of them. Madly attractive, isn't he. Oh well, better luck next time, Louise."

They were married in April, in a registry office with a few friends present. May had not had to consult her family because she had no family; she had lost her parents in a car accident when she was fifteen and had been brought up by her grandmother in Stamford, Connecticut. Her grandmother had died two years ago.

She felt it only proper, even distractedly in love with him as she was, to ask Cosmo a little about his background. His father, he told her, had died when he was an infant. His mother, who was a music teacher, of French descent, had remarried John Fane, an engineer. He had been brought up in New York, and after his formal education spent several years at the Paris Conservatory, when family circumstances forced him to go to work and make his own way. His mother was dead, and he was estranged from his father, who had in his turn remarried a wealthy Peruvian woman ("Don't ask me about our falling out, it is too painful a memory, perhaps later . . ."). It sounded rather sad, and glamorous, and a suitable history for Cosmo.

She had to take his talk of music and musicians, his showing her the completed pages of the first movement of his symphony, on faith. She knew very little about classical music, and had only accepted Louise's invitation to the concert at Carnegie Hall because it was to be followed by the party. She had the layman's awe of a mysterious and majestic world unto itself.

They decided to start off in her apartment, which was roomy, comfortable and rent-controlled, on Ninety-first Street between Lexington and Third. He confessed to a dark little studio arrangement on Staten Island. "No place for you, my May-rose." In addition to the usual living room, bedroom, bath and kitchen at May's, there was a small room, a den of sorts, which she had used as a sewing room. This, refurbished, became Cosmo's workroom, into which his rather shabby grand piano was moved. It was understood that when he had closed the door he was to be left undisturbed before he opened it again.

Of course, he was away a great deal on his symphony orchestra circuit, always calling her every night from wherever he was. Sometimes he brought back a handsome sum of money and sometimes very little. "I had thought three performances, four, and it turned out to be only one."

May's salary was good, and they lived comfortably if not luxuriously.

She thought herself very happy for the first year or so. Cosmo treated her with tenderness and passion. She was given a crash course in music and found it, she told him, "enriching." He was a marvelous cook and when he was at home, between concerts, often prepared a little feast of a dinner, although the ingredients were rather on the expensive side: lobster, Dover sole, rack of lamb, the choicest fruits and vegetables in and out of season, fine wines and brandies not only to drink but to flavor his sauces and desserts.

She had once murmured about the cost, and his large dark eyes grew sorrowful. "Oh May! You taunt me for choosing to stay with the most important work in my lifetime instead of going out and getting a . . ." Swift end to her murmuring.

After a time she began to chafe a little, on weekends, when he was immured in his room often four or five hours at a stretch. Once, passing close to the door, she heard what sounded like the chink of glass against glass. Did he *drink* in there? May wasn't anti-liquor; she looked forward to her own Manhattan, mixed and waiting for her when she got home from work.

It became increasingly evident that, yes, he did drink in there, and perhaps a lot. The strain of composing his symphony? She sought for patience, but sometimes his face and voice, when he emerged, frightened her a little.

His concert engagements began to lengthen, often to well over a week, but he seemed to be being paid less well than before. Once, when he shed his topcoat after returning from Pittsburgh, she caught from the covert cloth an unmistakeable waft of Chanel Number 5.

Could he possibly be . . . could there be other women? . . . no, never. Although musicians, temperaments, things like that . . . Could that, could they, be the reason for the increasingly long and less profitable engagements out of New York?

In her professional capacity, she was an able, aware and intelligent woman. One rainy Sunday in August, when Cosmo was in Wilmington, she sat looking down at the umbrellas six floors below, the cars, the taxis and buses, the busy world, people doing things and going places. Without summoning it up or thinking her way to it, an objective theory formed in her mind. What a good setup it would be, for a handsome man not overfond of work and liking a constant change of scene, a change of faces (women's): to woo and marry a pleasant compliant woman, pleasantly and steadily paid, with a pleasant apartment to move into and return to whenever he chose to do so.

Meals, delicious meals, to be had there, a quiet place to work when and if he wanted to work, and that rarest of commodities, financial security like a warm solid roof over all the rest of it.

Louise: "After you left he buttonholed me, wanting to know everything about you . . . everything."

Was this to be her life, the unvarying pattern of her whole future?

Or was it just a fantasy brought on by loneliness, and missing him, and the dark cold rainy afternoon?

She got up from her chair, went to the telephone, and

asked four friends to dinner. She went out and bought flowers for the table, and turned on pop music to cook by and have a party with. Her unexpected party was fun, and instead of her usual single Manhattan she had two and a half. Leaving with his wife shortly after midnight, one of her guests said, "Marriage has certainly done wonders for May. I've never seen her looking so well, and so merry."

After that, the erosion of the marriage was rapid.

Sent home one morning in early September by Mr. Connister, who considered his executive secretary invaluable, a perfect prize among secretaries—"I don't like that rasp in your throat and your face is very flushed. Go home and drink hot tea and rum and lemon, May, and go to bed."—she arrived at the apartment before noon and was getting out her key when she heard, from the living room, voices, laughter. Cosmo's and a woman's voice, light, pretty, teasing. "As you drink only champagne, I'll have to go out and get another bottle," said Cosmo.

May, without a moment's thought, fled down the corridor and into the elevator. She had never been any good at personal combat, confrontations, verbal violence interchanged; she was always caught short and rendered helpless by panicky tears. She went, shivering, to two movies in a row, finally had something to eat, tea and toast at a Schrafft's, and then went home at her usual hour.

Cosmo hadn't bothered to wash the ashtrays or wash up the two champagne flutes in the sink. There were also the remains of lunch, four plates, avocado peelings on the counter. May asked him if he'd been entertaining at lunch and he said yes, a young pianist who was down on his luck and needed cheering.

Their own little feasts had been discontinued several months before when, presented with roast partridges stuffed with cherries, preceded by a soufflé of oysters

black-grained on top with caviar, she had spoken, this
time above a murmur, about expenses. "With the money
we spend on food, I may have to give up my cleaning
woman." "And have me tie on an apron and do the
vacuuming and dusting and whatever else cleaning persons do?" Cosmo had asked savagely. "I get your message.
What about canned corned beef hash tomorrow night?"

In late September, he came home from three days in
Philadelphia without a cent to show for his performance
there. "I had to lend it all—and it is only a loan—to a
friend in really desperate need."

Turn, worm, said May to herself. "And," she asked, "was
she fun, your friend?" He gave her a glare in which she
seemed to read astonishment, stormed out of the apartment, and didn't come back until the next morning.

Those were some of the surface things. It was the draining away, subterranean, that was doing the real under-
mining. Do I *care* about any of this, May was asking herself. Does it matter? Wasn't I much happier before
Cosmo? Do I even know what I feel, or even who I am?
He is whittling away some core, some center, that I don't
think I can live without.

Dressed and ready to leave for Chicago one October
afternoon, a Saturday, he said, "May, I must have a thousand dollars, I haven't time to explain now. There isn't
that much in our checking account. Would you draw some
sort of draft, or whatever it is, that I could take to your
firm's office in Chicago Monday morning? I'm sure they'd
honor it, against your salary or some such arrangement."

"No," May said. "No, Cosmo, I will not." A different
May, who didn't know herself any longer, but in whose
voice the words formed themselves unanswerably.

But he did have an answer. He put down his cello case,
walked to her, and struck her hard against her mouth and

cheek. She fell backward, and her head hit the curved walnut arm of the cane-backed desk chair.

When she recovered consciousness, she found by the clock that she had only been out six or seven minutes. The apartment was silent. She got dazedly to her feet and went into the bathroom. Her upper lip was split and bleeding. The back of her head hurt badly, but she could, fingering through her hair, find no blood. She felt the tooth under the split place on her lip and found it loosened.

After washing her face, she put disinfectant and a flesh-colored strip bandage on her cut, combed her hair, looked steadily at herself in the mirror, at May Fane who used to be May Morris, who used to be someone else.

Moving without pauses, without tears, she got out her large suitcase from the hall closet, and the smaller matching one. She packed in under an hour. There were things she would have to leave behind, but she didn't really care; most of the leavings were Cosmo's clothes, bought in the last year or so, expensive, and after all not her own style.

So that Cosmo would have no grounds to set up an official search for her, police and so on—"My God, my wife's disappeared, she may have been kidnapped, or had an accident of some kind."—she wrote him a brief note. "I am leaving you to your amusements, and for good, Cosmo, so don't trouble to look around for me. The apartment rent is paid through the end of October. May."

It was then six o'clock. She went to the Lexington Hotel, a good distance downtown from the apartment (probably unnecessary, because he had told her his Chicago engagement would last for four or five days) and checked in under the new name that would be hers from now on, her grandmother's maiden name, Lockett. She did not wish to be seen as an unmarried woman and the term Ms. had not yet surfaced, so she chose for the registry card Mrs. George Lockett.

She was a little self-conscious about the bandage on her lip. The clerk took a sharp look at it, but the face was calm, the voice quiet.

Sunday was a long day, mostly spent in her room. She wrote a note to Mr. Connister, which was a hard task and an unhappy one. It would have to sound absolutely final or he too, relying on her as he did, might make inquiries. A family emergency, she wrote, which had to be kept private, had suddenly arisen. She must leave New York immediately, and there was no possibility of her returning for many months or perhaps years. She recommended as her replacement a remarkably capable girl, Peggy Barlow, who had been her own trusted assistant. And she was terribly sorry about all this. After some hesitation, she ended the note with, "True regards from the bottom of my heart, May."

She had her meals sent up, and did considerable thinking about what her destination was to be. On Monday morning, she went to the Forty-second Street branch of her bank and took, in cash, seven hundred and fifty dollars, leaving seventy-eight dollars for him.

She also got a cashier's check for the entire contents of her own savings account, six thousand eight hundred dollars. Some unexamined instinct of prudence had, at the time of her marriage, suggested that she keep this account a secret. Perhaps because someday she might choose to surprise Cosmo with a bagful of sugarplums, a trip to Paris or Rome. Or perhaps it was that her grandmother had always held the firm belief that any woman should have something all her own to fall back upon, life being at best an uncertain affair.

After breakfasting at a drugstore counter in Grand Central Station, she took a train to Boston. Get off any beaten track, a good way off it. What would be better than Provincetown, Massachusetts, where she had spent several enjoyable vacation weeks when she was twenty-six. She didn't fancy the South, or the West, and thought an out-of-season town at the tip of Cape Cod an eminently sensible choice.

In South Station in Boston, she picked up a copy of the *Provincetown Advocate,* examined its classified columns, made a phone call, and then took the scheduled flight several hours later on Provincetown-Boston Airlines.

The Lilacs had offered several year-round small cottages as being available, with gas heat as well as fireplaces. They could be rented for the full year or on a month-to-month basis. She vaguely remembered bicycling past the inn and thinking how attractive it looked.

That evening, having been provided with a few basic food supplies by Miss Winthrop, the owner and proprietor of the Lilacs, she cooked a dinner of tomato soup and buttered toast in her own small sparkling kitchen and floated thankfully off to sleep in her own blessed single bed in her own new home.

Several weeks later, she was given an opportunity to try on her new identity. Miss Winthrop asked her to tea, at her house across the street from the inn.

In a normally polite, non-prying way, she asked what had brought Mrs. Lockett to Provincetown at this quiet season.

They were not then and for some time, and that only in private, on a first-name basis.

Mrs. Lockett said that her husband George, a mining engineer, had died in an accident at the site in Colorado, and that she had returned to New York a few months afterwards and been offered her old position as secretary to a firm of lawyers. Then the elderly man she had worked for had passed away, said Mrs. Lockett. She had felt she needed a change, and remembered a pleasant time spent on vacation in Provincetown, even remembered passing by the Lilacs and admiring the inn.

She volunteered the information that, after a bit, she thought she might try to find a job here, perhaps something with the Chamber of Commerce, or the Town Hall.

Sipping Darjeeling tea, Miss Winthrop had said with the same polite interest, "You type, then? And I assume know something about figures, and managing things, and so on."

"Oh, yes indeed."

A week later, during the second shared tea by the fire, Miss Winthrop said, "As is perfectly clear, I am a good deal older than you are. I've been running this place by myself for ten years. I wonder if you'd consider a job as my assistant. You strike me as an efficient woman, and amiable enough to turn to—as I always have, when it's needed—in the kitchen, or wherever fill-in functioning is required."

Mrs. Lockett deliberately allowed herself a minute or so for thought. Then she said, "I have a feeling, Miss Winthrop, that there is nothing I would like better."

THREE

The Lilacs had been built, and soundly built, in 1830. It had originally been a farmhouse, but the farmer must have been a man of taste and means, to judge from the paneling, the graceful carved mantelpieces, the wainscoting, the finely turned stair rails and banisters.

It might have been taken for a private residence except for the inn sign above the gate, lettered in black on an oval white board. Not a large house, but an ample one, with a wing on one side added later. The clapboards were painted a soft lavender blue, and the woodwork and shutters were white. The modest garden, which with its flowers Miss Winthrop had planted, looked like a work of embroidery, curved on the left along the brick path to the front door.

In back was a well-kept lawn ending in a broad stone terrace directly over the water of Cape Cod Bay. Stone steps led down from the center of the terrace into the water, or at low tide to the sand. Old wind-twisted willows on the lawn gave shade to those who wanted it. Miss Winthrop loathed anything that smacked of quaint and ye-olde; the knowing visitor, however, was aware of pleasant amenities long missing from the contemporary American architectural scene, an easy and natural elegance wherever the eye fell.

At least fifty per cent of its clientele were visitors who came back every summer, making when they departed reservations for the following year. A room and bath here cost no more, and often a little less, than at the Best Western, or the Holiday Inn, or other large motel-hotels, but then the Lilacs wasn't everybody's idea of a resort hotel. No swimming pool, no bar, no room service, and only breakfast served, although it was a generous and delicious breakfast, included in the price of accommodations.

On regaining the security of her office, and her daily tasks, Mrs. Lockett tried to regain herself after the awful shock at the hotdog stand on Commercial Street.

Fortunately, there was work to do, guests to be registered and shown to their rooms. There was no desk or counter in the entrance sitting room; all inn business was conducted in Mrs. Lockett's office, of which the door always stood wide open. Here you registered, bought stamps, picked up folders on local holiday activities, sought any information you wished, got change if you needed it, borrowed beach towels, and then paid your bill when, usually with regret, you left.

Mrs. Lockett resisted a strong impulse to close the door, close herself in her room, safe and unseen, with her familiar world enfolding her.

The inn was by now two-thirds full and she had no time for an hour or so to face fears that had set up a deep interior trembling all through her body. Or to pose questions to herself for which answers must be found. Or to decide, after rational exploration of the whole thing, that there was really nothing to worry about. Nothing at all.

As on most dark days threatening rain, the sitting room was a popular place. It was comfortably furnished in white wicker and chintz sofas and chairs, with well-filled bookcases, an inlaid walnut card table, and the rose and green dhurrie Miss Winthrop always had put down in summer to spare her Mahal. The paneled walls were painted gray-green. A good fire crackled on the hearth, which Maria

Captiva had lit when she noticed during Mrs. Lockett's absence that the temperature had not gone up, from 65 degrees, but down, to 61.

When it was getting on for two o'clock, Mrs. Lockett realized that she had had no lunch and thought food and hot tea might help the inner quivering like a pulse beating all over her body.

Sitting by the window in her own room, with the door locked and bolted, she nibbled at a cream cheese and olive sandwich and drank deeply her hot sweet tea.

Well, begin. Think.

Start with the easy, the best solution. That he had come over for the day on the Boston excursion boat, and would be departing in under two hours. How had he been dressed for his day's outing? She closed her eyes and found she had taken, in those few seconds, a mental photograph exact in every detail.

Head bare, hair still thick, the dark streaked with gray, longish but not in any neglected-looking way. Beard, new to her eye. Carriage not quite as erect, shoulders heavier now, stooping a little. Turtleneck cable-knit sweater, jeans, dark blue espadrilles, bare ankles. (But for some years now, clothing told you nothing about the wearer's status or income.) He had put on weight, but the body still suggested power. Had he any kind of luggage, say a duffel bag at his feet? No. Did that corroborate the day-trip theory, or did it mean the opposite, that he was staying somewhere in town?

If he hadn't come and would blessedly leave on the Boston boat, where in town was he likely to be staying? The Lilacs would be at a far remove from the kind of lodging he would choose. He'd want some shiny, showy place with lots of nearly naked girls stretched out on lounge chairs around the pool. But those places cost money. She had no idea if he had attached himself to an alternate source—or sources—of money after she fled.

Pulling herself up with a jerk, she forced herself to the awareness that she hadn't any idea what a sixty-year-old Cosmo would do, would want, would feel. No idea in what style he lived, or liked to live. She hadn't seen him for decades. How could you try to imagine the pattern of the doings of a total stranger?

In any case, what had she to fear, from Cosmo? True, they were still legally man and wife. At no point had the idea of divorce entered her mind. Instant flight and total secrecy were imperative. Divorce proceedings at the time would have brought her again into contact with him, pinned her down geographically at such-and-such an address, made her vulnerable, trackable.

Were wives, after a separation of decades, still responsible for their husbands' debts? Did the statute of limitations apply? Find out.

Or better still, dismiss this probably wholly unimportant glimpse of a visitor to Provincetown. Anybody and everybody was likely to pay a visit to Provincetown in summer.

Yes, dismiss it, and do that right away. It was a form of madness to sit here spinning nightmares for herself.

He didn't know her name. If, in any conversation, a mention of Mrs. Lockett of the Lilacs came up, it would mean nothing to him.

It would be only common sense, however, to avoid the center of town for a few days. Putting everything in rational perspective, it would be unpleasant to meet him face-to-face on the street. But just unpleasant; nothing more.

Now, she told herself firmly, you've thought it out and got it straight.

Close the book on this meaningless little incident, the fleeting presence of Cosmo.

Having calmed and cheered herself in her own way, she ate with pleasure a chocolate eclair she had bought for tonight's dinner. Delicious.

It was the consensus among the regular guests that, while Miss Winthrop was very much missed, they were lucky that Mrs. Lockett conducted the inn in a manner identical to Miss Winthrop's.

On a sunlit noon, two of the guests sat on the broad stone steps leading down from the terrace. It was half-tide, and the bottom step was under water. They were drinking martinis mixed by Mrs. Gage, who had found Mrs. Brown in the sitting room reading a magazine and said, "Come out and have some booze, Jane, instead of wasting this lovely day indoors."

There was no ice machine at the Lilacs, but Mrs. Captiva always kept ample supplies of ice cubes ready in the freezer. The lack of a bar was considered by many something of an advantage; so much cheaper to get your supplies from the liquor store a short distance away.

The two women had arrived yesterday and were renewing last year's friendship. Glasses clinked. "Cheers, Lois. Who owns the place now? Whoever it is was smart to keep Mrs. Lockett on. When I read Miss Winthrop had died, I thought, oh God, there goes the Lilacs and maybe we'll have to try the Hamptons this summer, or Mount Desert Island."

"Mrs. Lockett owns it, or so I've heard, the whole caboodle left to her by Miss W. What a delicious martini. And to think it would have cost us, just the one I mean, at least two seventy-five in a bar."

"What a plum to have dropped into her lap, but I suppose she's earned it. I gather she's been here since the Year One."

"I wonder," Lois Gage said, "if she got all that marvelous loot Miss W. showed me once, as she knew I'm in the antiques business. A service for one hundred in lobster-pattern Royal Worcester, a Queen Anne tea service, shelves full of old silver and glass—not inn stuff but family things. The Virginia branch of the Winthrops must have been quite splendid at one time. Worth a fortune, those things of hers. I must ask Mrs. Lockett if they're still in her house."

"Well, the inn and land and her house and the cottages are worth a fortune twice over," Jane Brown said. "Let us hope and pray she hangs onto it forever and ever."

In a pleasant bedroom over the terrace and the bay, Maria Captiva and Susan Perry were bed-making and tidying. Mrs. Lockett followed her predecessor's practice in liking her girls to work in pairs. She had no doubts about Maria's perfect honesty; Maria, in Boston College now, had worked summers at the Lilacs since she was sixteen. But Susan was new, in fact had just started today. She looked all right, she looked quite nice, with her almond-shaped striking blue eyes, her rose-tinted tan, casually curly dark hair, long throat and soft South Carolina voice, a voice that suggested to Mrs. Lockett a nice family background. But you never knew.

Susan, Maria thought, was a bit slow, right now at first, but she'd pick up speed. Plumping a bed pillow, she asked, "Have you done this kind of work before, summers?"

"Yes, once, a few years back, in Nantucket," Susan said, plumping the pillow on her side of the bed. "When I came up here in June I thought I could make more money at something else and took a job at the Caper. You know, that open-front hotdog stand near MacMillan Wharf."

"Oh, yes. Buggie's place." Maria grinned. "Everybody knows Buggie. Not everybody likes him, though."

"I fear I am one of them, the latter. How is Mrs. Lockett, to work for? She seems a very nice woman." Two weeks before, she had bicycled to the Lilacs, which she thought one of the prettiest places in town, and on impulse went in and asked in the office if summer help was needed. It was; Mrs. Lockett was in the process of making calls to likely girls. Susan looked to her very likely indeed. Susan told her she had a job, had had one since she came up in early June from Lilith, South Carolina, but that it didn't suit.

"And what job is that?"

"At the Caper, serving hotdogs and hamburgers and soft drinks. I'm well paid, and I don't mind the work, but it's very bad when night comes along." In her southern way of putting things more formally and delicately than her northern sisters, she said, "There are a great many intoxicated men stopping at the stand offering me unwanted invitations."

"Oh dear. Very wise of you to look elsewhere." After a brief probe into Susan's background, age (twenty-four), marital status (unmarried), and experience working in this line (Murdoch House in Nantucket), it was agreed that she report for work on July first.

Maria, in answer to the question about their employer, said, "She's all right to work for, doesn't peck and heckle, but don't be misled by her cozy looks. She expects good work and no skimping. She takes a dim view of the help calling in sick and always suspects—and she's usually right —that it's a hangover. Miss W's rule, which she'll follow, is that after three sick call-ins, you're out. Like three strikes. We make our own lunch in the kitchen, whenever we get time to eat it, what with some people hanging around in bed until noon, and have it at the kitchen table. Now, you take the bathroom and I'll do the vacuuming. Then we'll switch bath and vacuum in the next room."

In the next room, peacefully blue and white but remarkably untidy, Maria called from the bathroom, "Oh God, this tub. She must have poured a bucketful of bath oil into the water. Will you get me that big box of Tide from the cart?"

Coming out ten minutes later, palm pressed to the small of her back, she said, "Talking about hangovers, I've got a killer. When I bend over there are crazy little silver sparkles swimming all around my head."

Susan nodded sympathetically. "Vertigo. Was it worth collecting your hangover, did you have a nice time?"

"Did I ever! My chum sprang for the Lightship, maybe you've been there, one of the best places in town, but usually jammed."

She went to the cleaning cart outside the door, took her large handbag from a drawer at the bottom, and from it extracted a frosty can of beer. "Will you keep watch for me, Susan? I'd offer you some but I need it all. One-thirty, it was, when we left the Lightship last night. Close the door all but an inch or so."

She took a deep grateful gulp from the can. "They have a new piano player there, Cosmo Something, not young but can he ever play. When the dinner crowd thinned out he began taking requests, and he played two of my favorite songs." A pause for another gulp. "My friend sent him a drink to thank him, and he came over to our table and sat with us for a little while. Kind of a haggard romantic type but much too old for me. We asked if this was just a guest appearance, but he said, no, he's here for the summer. Get your next date to take you there if only for a late drink. Can he ever play!"

FOUR

Mrs. Oliva's Bayview Lodge was halfway up Lisbon Lane, one of the many short connecting streets running from Bradford to Commercial, the two main arteries of the town, referred to by its natives as Back and Front Streets. In spite of its name, which sounded promising, the Bayview was a shabby white clapboard house with a rusty-screened front porch, a brief strip of lawn in front given over mainly to the cultivation of dandelions, and a raggedy privet hedge. For those who wished to stretch their pennies, it was a useful place to lay your head at night.

At ten o'clock on Saturday morning, a clap of pain in his right temple woke Cosmo Fane in his small room on the top floor. From this elevation, there actually was a view of the bay. A hideous blare of sunlight from the two windows made his eyes as well as his head ache.

He groaned aloud, consulted his watch, rolled himself upward and tentatively placed his feet on the rag rug. When, last night, had he gotten to bed? He had no recollection of climbing the outside stairway to the top-floor rooms and using his key and getting himself to bed. After finishing up at the Lightship at two, he had dropped in here and there for a final drink, and then another final drink.

The sound of a guitar being played in the next room rang through his nerve ends. Under his windows two young men were quarreling loudly about whose turn it was to wear the pink-and-white-striped pants.

He was lucky in finding the bathroom shared by the three third-floor rooms empty. He swallowed two aspirins from the bottle in his bathrobe pocket and, looking with distaste at the soiled tub, settled for a quick wash at the sink with a well-used cake of soap in a gummy plastic dish. One of the white towels looked almost all right to dry off with.

See how his expenses went, food and so on, see how tips went, and maybe he could move out of this hole into something a little better. Buggie had recommended it to him as the cheapest place to be had in the center of town. He had only moved in on Wednesday, that night being his first at the piano in the Lightship. He was to play there Monday through Friday, and then fill his Nantucket engagement on weekends, when the Lightship featured triplets, the We Three, pretty girls with long blond hair, two at the piano and one at the harp.

In the course of arranging his Provincetown job, Cosmo heard on the musical grapevine that a cellist was wanted at the Admiralty in Nantucket. He auditioned in late May and was promptly signed up. He would be playing there, for the third weekend, tonight.

His face in the mirror was not encouraging. Christ, he thought, I look like my own grandfather. But he wasn't unduly worried; he knew the elastic fashion in which during the day he could spring back, shed years, look not bad at all, look pretty damned good. Get some sun, get a lot of sun, that ought to do it.

He put on jeans and an expensive silk pongee shirt given to him nine years ago by a woman he had lived with briefly in Flagstaff, Arizona. He couldn't remember her full name, Elouise Something, but he still had the shirt; good silk lasts.

The guitar next door was still at it. Cosmo glanced at his cello case leaning in a corner of the room and thought, with a nervous flick of savagery, I'll show him what he's up against. He took out his cello and sitting right against the dividing wall began on Saint-Saëns' Cello Concerto Number 1 in A minor, choosing as his style an excruciating mishandling and souring of notes. He stopped in the middle and played one bar seven times, making it sound worse and more painful to the ear as he went along. His cello on command produced noises like the last groans of a dying elephant. After the seventh bar repeat, he stopped and listened.

The guitar was silent. Cosmo, his spirits already lifted, grinned, teeth flashing white over the dark beard that he kept well trimmed with his own deft scissors.

He had an outdoor breakfast at a cafe, under a blue umbrella, his usual three cups of black coffee and then, when he could face food, a poached egg on an English muffin.

Continue with the first priority of the day, to get himself in shape for this evening. The manager of the Admiralty liked his Wistaria Room string quartet in black tie, on tune, and sober.

He was not interested in sailing, swimming, tennis, croquet, bicycling or any of the other sports available here. He thought all joggers and runners madmen courting heart failure, and was not very enthusiastic about walking, but walking in the sun would have to be his cure for the time being. Strolling the crowded sidewalks, hands in his pockets, it occurred to him that walking with an object, a destination, would make it easier to take.

A purpose just might be that girl, Maria Captiva. Indian-tanned, glistening long dark hair, dark brown eyes with a dazzle in them from the thick dripping candle stuck in a rum bottle at the table in the Lightship. While he was having a drink with her and her escort, he had asked where she worked, and she had said—what? Something to do with flowers, something to do with spring. The Lilacs.

It was all very well to have Nutmeg, in Nantucket, on tap for weekends, but Monday to Friday was a long time to spend without the various pleasures of female company. She looked young, not more than twenty or so, but ripe-young, in fact too much of a handful for that red-headed string bean of a kid who was footing the bill.

He asked a policeman directing traffic which way to the Lilacs and was told, with a gesture of the arm, to walk that way along Commercial Street until he got almost to the end of it, and he couldn't miss the Lilacs. "There's a big hedge of them, nothing like it in town, old as God, something to see in late May," the policeman added enthusiastically. "All bloomed out by now, of course."

Provincetown is probably one of the last places in the nation, or indeed on earth, where the pedestrian is still king. Vacationers sipping their morning coffee from containers, eating ice cream cones, greeting and gossiping, overflowed into the narrow street or wandered across at random while cars crawled, waited, then crawled again.

But once clear of the center of town and the strolling crowd, composed notably of young men and young women in pairs, the sidewalks were quiet. You were back in a New England seaside village, with a blaze of sunlit water to your left. A creature of cities, Cosmo saw without any particular stirrings of pleasure the houses with their little lawns and gardens close to the street, white clapboard, red-painted clapboard, shingles salted to silver, the white picket fences, trees ballooning fresh and full in the light wind, orange day lilies in their trumpeting clumps and borders, roses mixing their scent with the breath of the bay.

When he came to the bend in the road where on the bay side a complex of peculiar-looking converted houses stood, a woman coming toward him stopped and said a soft, "Good morning." Cosmo stopped too, politely. She waved an arm at the building complex. "Do you know what the Coast Guard's new quarters cost? Eighteen million dollars. So ugly, don't you think. And their old quarters were perfectly serviceable." This was not said belligerently, but in a pensive tone.

She was a woman of perhaps seventy, with an oval, delicately lined face and gray hair parted in the center and knotted at the back. She gave Cosmo the impression, in her appearance and clothing, of a gentle and educated Quakerism.

He was aware that the fine dark eyes were studying his face with a quickening of interest. "Now what do I connect you with?" she asked, not intrusively. "Music. Yes. The forehead and eyes. I do remember them, but I don't *think* you wore a beard."

Oh God, what's she caught me out in, Cosmo thought, horrified.

She went on, moving softly and without effort into the past. "Oh yes, twenty or so years ago, in Philadelphia. A musical afternoon at Mrs. Toogood's, on Delancey Street, wasn't it? Dear Mr. Ormandy was expected but he was detained at the Academy. But some of his Philadelphia Orchestra men gave us such a beautiful little private concert. I remember your cello. Oh, and you, of course. Are you still playing?"

"Yes," Cosmo said, "still playing." He felt the hot color coming up under his skin. Not in symphony orchestras, though, madam. Struck off everybody's list nine or ten years ago for rehearsals, not quite sober, or careless and unprepared at rehearsals, or not turning up for rehearsals at all. A fill-in no longer wanted by any conductor or manager anywhere.

"Well, I must be on my way," the woman said. "So

pleasant of you to have brought that afternoon back to me." She drifted past him with a little smile.

Cosmo continued on his way, became aware of the forward stoop of his shoulders, and momentarily straightened his spine. It was cooler here, on the rim of town. The light wind quickened and chilled him. He should have worn his sweater.

How far did this damned street run? Was there any end to it? He climbed a rise, panting with the effort, and descending it saw on his left the lilac hedge and the white signboard. He walked to the picket gate in the arch and looked in. Maria, if she worked here, would hardly be disporting herself on the lawn.

A military-looking man came down the brick path toward him and opened the gate. "Nice place, isn't it," he said complacently. "Full up, I'm afraid." He closed the gate and began walking briskly toward the town center.

Cosmo leaned in over the waist-high pickets and saw near him, weeding the flower border, a solid yet supple young man, deeply tanned, with dark hair spilling to his hooked eyebrows over dark eyes, a high-cheekboned face somehow familiar.

Cosmo asked him casually, "Is Maria on today?"

The young man looked him over carefully and thoroughly, not rising from his knees. "Yes, who wants to know?"

"A friend of hers. We met last night. Cosmo."

"Oh well, too bad, visitors aren't allowed during working hours. Beds have to be made and linen changed and scrubbing up to do." He seemed to deliver this ultimatum with pleasure.

"Where does she live, do you know?"

"With her ma and as a matter of fact mine too. Snow Street."

"What's her day off, or days?"

"Varies from week to week according to work load," still deliberately unhelpful.

"Well, thanks." Possessive type of brother, Cosmo thought, perhaps it was a Portuguese trait, protecting the womenfolk from invading males. Let it, let Maria, go for the moment, follow it up later. In the meantime, force himself to walk another half mile or so and then turn back. His legs, unaccustomed to walking distances, felt weary but the rest of him felt better, coming around nicely.

Going into the kitchen for a drink of water, Dominic Captiva found Maria having a late-morning cup of coffee at the table. "A man stopped at the gate looking for you. I told him you were on duty and he left," he told her between deep gulps of cold water. "Named Cosmo, didn't give his last name, met you last night."

"Oh. Mmmm." Maria's expression was that of one flattered and pleased, and a little amused. "He plays the piano at the Lightship. He's terrific."

"Maybe terrific, but too old to go chasing kids, and he looked, I don't know, he looked to me like bad news."

"Maybe," Maria said demurely, "he wanted to give me a private concert."

Going out at the door, Dominic said, "He didn't look like what he had in mind was playing the piano."

Commercial Street ended, turning into a wide asphalted road that curved between pines. Cosmo soon reached, on his right, a large motel and restaurant, called the Moors. He thought he had earned himself a drink, to say the least, and went to the bar, where he was by no means alone; a good deal of drink and merriment was going on. For safety, he limited himself to one double whiskey, to which he added a small dash of water.

Refreshed, he started on his walk back to Lisbon Lane. Approaching the Lilacs again, he slowed, thinking Maria might emerge to sweep the brick walk, or perhaps to carry trash across the street to the wooden bins at one side of the small parking lot.

Looking through the arch, he saw the front door open. He moved, instantly and without any thought at all, to the left, where the lilacs concealed him but he could still see in on a slant.

Closing the door behind her was a pink and white woman, gray-haired, a bit plump, in a pale blue dress sprigged with green. She was carrying a pewter pitcher. She turned to her left and went across the grass toward where two other women were sitting in white webbed lawn chairs with paperbacks in their hands, in the shade of the old twisted willows beside the house.

"Would anyone care to join me in a refill of iced tea? It's just made fresh," her voice floated, over the lawn, and over the decades, to Cosmo.

FIVE

Cosmo had plenty of time, on Saturday afternoon, to muse about the jolting sight of his wife.

He drove himself in the black Ford Escort he had rented on Tuesday to Hyannis, where he left his car in a parking lot near the dock and boarded the three-thirty ferry to Nantucket, carrying his cello case.

The ferry would get into Nantucket about seven, which was cutting it rather fine; but he kept his dress clothes at Margaret's, and her house was not far from the Admiralty, where he was due at eight.

When they had been discussing arrangements for the summer, in New York, in April, Buggie had said, "Better get around by bus, you won't need a car." "Why shouldn't I have a car? I am not a bus person." "Well, you might get into some kind of accident, lots of crazy drivers around when the season starts, police on the scene poking in and around and all that." "Unless you care to hire me an armor-plated Rolls-Royce with a getaway kind of chauffeur, a car I will have." He was not, then or at any time, going to be under Buggie's thumb.

Not one to court the forces of nature in powerful doses, the strong winds and unimpeded sun of the popular open-top deck, he sat on one of the long cushioned wall benches of the spacious main deck, which was relatively un-crowded. There was plenty to see through the big open windows if you were interested in that sort of thing: the sailboats and power launches and Windsurfers; the Hyannis Port compound of the Kennedy family to the right, soon after you pulled away from the dock; the umbrella-starred beaches, the brisk choppy blue of Nantucket Sound. Cosmo was not inclined to seasickness, but a lot of other people evidently were; whenever a whistle blew, young men in white with mops and pails came and went running.

For the tenth time, he returned mentally to the lawn at the Lilacs. Well, what about it? Why shouldn't she be staying at a nice place by the water on vacation? Or maybe she was retired. She had always made good money, she had the secure contented look of the well employed, or the possessor of a comfortable income.

He knew absolutely nothing of her life since she had left him. He had never tried to find her, never even considered it. At the time, he thought that on the whole he had had a pretty good run for his money. And a few months before that final afternoon, he had seen that the thing was beginning to fall irretrievably apart. All right, he had taken her for a bit more soft, more gullible than she actually was, but still there had been sixteen months of freedom and comfort with her.

Another reason that he had not contemplated, when he found her note, taking some kind of furious pursuit was that he had been haunted, the first few days in Chicago, by the fear that he might have killed her when he struck her and she fell against the desk chair, her head whacking the arm. Broken her neck. He was away from New York for a week, saw nothing in the New York papers he combed every day, and was not contacted by the Chicago police. But would the death by violence of an executive secretary even make the papers?

When he did return to the apartment, he went stealthily in through the tradesmen's entrance in case there might be a police watch on the front entrance. In view of his midnight terrors about manslaughter, the emptiness of the apartment, even the note, came as a form of relief.

He couldn't very well stay at the apartment for the paid-up month because their friends would be telephoning in the normal way, or dropping in. He wanted no part of the scalding business of saying, no, May wasn't here, she had left him. No point in lying about an extended visit to someone in her family; she had no family.

The next day, taking the telephone off the hook, he removed anything he thought to be of value, anything that could be carried without help, from the silver flatware to the old Bristol glass clock to the collection of paperweights May had been gathering since she was eighteen; and a good deal more besides. Carrying his booty in the largest of his suitcases, he made three trips to a west side storage warehouse, planning to put these items up for sale in the next few weeks.

Before returning to Staten Island to stay with the friend who had accommodated him there for the six months prior to his marriage, he wrote a brief note to the manager of the apartment building. In it he said that their family income had stopped and they were unable to remain there, and that he was sure there would be no trouble in immediately renting these desirable premises. If they got indignant about that, he told himself, the lease still with six months to go, there wasn't much they could do about it. They were welcome to the furniture, but there was nothing else to attach, of his. He kept his small secret bank account under another name—his real name, Harold Fane. He had adopted "Cosmo" at the age of fifteen.

The idea of divorcing her for desertion, then and at any later time, never even crossed his mind. Trouble, expense, and for what? Being, officially, a married man offered certain conveniences, especially in encounters with women when they started thinking about permanence, about marriage.

Well, it was all in the past. Maybe it hadn't been she at the door with the pitcher of iced tea. Most people had doubles. He had once, himself, to his great displeasure, been mistaken by a woman on a plane for her hairdresser of several years back. "Nobody's ever given me an Apollo cut like yours, where are you working now? Even if it's a thousand miles from New York I'd—" and then at his glare, "Oh, sorry, I could have sworn you were . . . Sorry."

Doubles. He saw before his eyes the figure in the sprigged blue dress become two, standing in front of two doors. He swung his legs up onto the bench, rested his head on his cello case, and went soundly off to sleep.

His taxi took him in a spine-jolting fashion up cobble-stoned Main Street, past the superb houses, many of which had been built for whaling captains. Cosmo had developed an immediate fondness for Nantucket because it looked so authentically like money, real money, from the fortune in boats tied up at the marina to the soaring of white columns supporting noble pediments to the silver-plated knockers and doorknobs of the great Starbuck houses they were passing now, known as the Three Bricks.

The moors began abruptly, higher than the town. The cottage at which the taxi deposited its passenger did not reek of money, which is why he had rented his room there in the first place. It was comfortable, though, in more ways than one, built of weather-silvered cedar shingles, with white-painted trim and white window boxes full of nasturtiums.

He went up the porch steps, tried the knob of the front door, found it locked, and opened it with his key. The locked door puzzled him because Margaret's green Buick was parked in the sandy driveway. A note left for him on the coffee table cleared this up. "Cosmo dear, I'm off to the Embroidery Club for the evening, I had a friend pick me up so I could leave the car for you. I may stop by at the Admiralty later, and we can drive home together. Chicken sandwich for you in the refrigerator if you have time to snatch a bite, also a split of champagne. I hope it's a brand you like." The note was signed "Your Nutmeg."

It had taken a little more than two weeks for Mrs. Margaret Rudd to turn into Nutmeg. Looking for inexpensive lodgings, a rare commodity here, Cosmo had heard that a Mrs. Rudd had a spare room she usually rented out in summer, didn't ask a lot for it, what she really liked was someone in the house for company, and preferably a man, for protection.

The room was small but pleasant, Cosmo found; he also found while discussing arrangements with Mrs. Rudd in her living room that he was in the promising presence of a sitting duck.

Over tea and cookies, she told him a little about herself. She was a widow of four years. She and Mr. Rudd, who had been in the construction business, lived in a big house in Lynn, Massachusetts, which six months after his death she sold. She now lived all year in this holiday cottage of theirs. "But it does get lonely. That's why, summers, I rent out the guestroom, it's not that I really need the money, but it's nicer that way if the person is nice." She underlined this qualification with a wide, welcoming smile.

She looked to be in her late forties, with a trim, rounded figure, discreetly fawn-brown hair just on the edge of wanting another coloring, a curly-lipped mouth and a dimpled chin.

Cosmo was aware that she was immediately attracted to him; perhaps mesmerized would put the case better. He explained that he only wanted the room on weekends, and told her why. Her face fell, and then, recovering, she said, "Well then, I'll take a third off the weekly rent, d'you think that would be fair? I wouldn't like to take an alternate roomer for the five other days, you wouldn't feel settled and at home, would you, of course you'd want your own things in your own closet and bureau drawers."

Cosmo said that was kind of her and would suit him very well, adding, "It's so nice to feel that one is in a real *home,* not a come-and-go place. Would you mind if I occasionally practice my cello?"

No, no, she would love it if he did. She adored music, although she didn't, she said, know much about it. Accepting a second cup of tea, he name-dropped a few symphony orchestras and their conductors. But, just so that she wouldn't get the idea that he was rolling in money, he went on to say that ill health had kept him off the concert stage for three years and he was just getting back into the swing now.

"Oh, poor dear"—with an anxiety and sympathy that were not at all motherly—"but if the way a person looks means anything you've got your health all back by now!"

"All back." He got up to stand towering over her. "I'll go and get my bag from the motel and move right in."

"You came in a taxi I saw, it's silly to call another one, I'll drive you there and back."

"But that's too much to ask of you, especially after so kindly adjusting my room rent to fit my temporarily flattened wallet . . ."

He soon found, as he had expected, there was very little that was too much to ask of Margaret Rudd.

The day after he took the room, he got up to find his landlady embroidering the hem of a pillowcase in the living room. She looked different than she had yesterday,

black sweater and white pants instead of the pink-flow-
ered shirtwaist dress she had then worn (the kind of dress
that reminded him vaguely of someone, some other
woman, long ago, who?) She had evidently seen to her
hair-coloring: there was no whisper of gray at the parting.
And more makeup, neatly applied, even a touch of mas-
cara on her eyelashes.

Oho, thought Cosmo to himself.

She smiled at him over her embroidery. "You look as if
you slept well. The air on the moors is . . . well, like
aspirin, only you don't get the acid reaction. Suppose I fix
you a bit of breakfast, I've already had mine."

She got up from her chair, and Cosmo, gazing deep into
her hazel eyes, said, "You are much too good to me."

Going into the big, well-equipped kitchen, followed by
him, she said, "No, it's fun. People around. I might say
special people around. Do you mind a little music with
your breakfast?" She switched on the kitchen radio and
Respighi's *The Pines of Rome* filled the room. Cosmo
made a bet with himself that she had set the dial the night
before at this classical music station.

She gave him scrambled eggs, grilled Canadian bacon,
and well-buttered cinnamon-raisin bread toast, with tomato juice first and a whole pot of fresh hot coffee. "You
cosmopolitan types, oh, sorry, no pun intended"—giggling—"probably eat much more glamorous things for
breakfast, but a square meal is a square meal anywhere."
She joined him at the kitchen table, watching with pleasure as he ate, and having another cup of coffee herself.

Cosmo told her that he wouldn't be starting his Provincetown engagement for several weeks and that he was
going to give himself a Nantucket holiday. "Will you show
me the town, if and when you're not busy doing other
things?"

His invariable rule of thumb in these encounters was:

When you're planning to take a lot, give a little back, but give it with a flourish.

They strolled the town for several hours, spending a lot of time at the marina looking over the ranks of boats tied up, every other boat looking as if its owner must be in possession of millions. There was even an oceangoing steam yacht with two slanting funnels.

Later, he bought them a splendid lunch at the Mad Hatter. "But your poor flattened wallet," she protested when he had ordered a vermouth cassis for her and a dry martini for himself. "For my generous hostess, nothing is too much," Cosmo said. "I'm in the mood for lobster thermidor, are you? Not to be eaten of course without a little splash of champagne, or Chablis if you don't like the bubbles."

When, at seven-thirty, he emerged from his room, black-tied and dinner-jacketed, carrying his cello case, her mouth fell open. "Oh, you look so . . . oh *heavens*. Now don't bother to call a taxi to take you to the Admiralty, I'll drive you."

It was during the playing of the Schubert String Quartet in B at around nine when, his cello being given a short silence, he glanced over the room, three-quarters full, candlelit, crystal-chandeliered, with spotlit wistaria vines trailing their bloom outside the long windows. He saw the party of four women being escorted to their table and seated by the headwaiter. Margaret Rudd, in a low-cut black-and-white flowered dress, caught his eye and waved to him. The score now demanded his return to the cello, and as he lowered his eyes he saw her bending right and left in excitement, smiling and gesticulating to her friends. He could pretty well guess what she was saying, "Yes, believe it or not, *that's* my new boarder. We had the nicest lunch at the Mad Hatter today, just the two of us . . ."

The fifth night of his stay was spent in her bedroom, in her bed.

It was on the eighth night, suddenly giggling at his hand on her half-asleep body, that she whispered, "Sometimes I laughed when, well, at certain points, when my husband and I . . . and that's when he made up his nickname for me, Nutmeg."

The night before he left for his first engagement at the Lightship, she said at four in the morning, "Look, paying me is silly, it makes me feel funny. Consider yourself my guest for the rest of the summer, Cosmo . . . darling Cosmo." And, laying two fingers against his protesting lips, "My, to say the least, honored guest."

On this weekend visit of the first Saturday of July, after five days' absence, Saturday night had turned into Sunday morning when Cosmo let himself into the cottage. He'd had a pleasant amusing time after the quintet played its last notes at eleven o'clock. The girl, who looked rather rich, asked him in a note delivered by a waiter if he'd like to join their little party, three men and one other girl. Their little party, in the bar at Totter's Tavern, went on for some time.

He felt a slight dread at the idea of confronting Margaret, a probably upset Margaret, but on the other hand a quantity of liquor had made him feel buoyant and confident.

She emerged from her, their, bedroom at the sound of the front door closing. She said in a sad muted voice, "I was so terribly worried about you, I thought of all sorts of things, particularly a car accident, three people were killed on the road to Quaise here Wednesday night. I thought about calling the police, but . . ."

Good. She had apparently decided that her approach this time was the useful: more in sorrow than in anger.

"I'm so sorry. I should have called." He took her in his arms and kissed her. "There was a late party in a private dining room at the Admiralty and we were asked—commanded, that is—to supply background music for the hiccups and the shouts of laughter. My poor Nutmeg, but it's never too late for love, is it?"

He was not, however, a man who liked the feel of a collar around his neck, and the first light tug on the leash.

On Sunday morning, after a late and lavish breakfast with an appeased Margaret, Cosmo took the car into town to buy the Sunday New York *Times* while Margaret did the dishes.

His speculations of yesterday, on the ferry coming over, returned to tease him. Passing a public telephone, he stopped on impulse, after getting from information the number of the Lilacs. If Maria Captiva answered, he would just hang up, she might remember his voice, but did it matter? Well, maybe it did. A voice that sounded elderly, with an accent that he had already come to recognize as Cape Cod, said, "The Lilacs, may I help you?"

"Yes, I'm trying to get in touch with Mrs. Fane. Is she staying there?"

After a short pause, while she apparently studied registrations, the woman said, "No, there's no one of that name here."

"But I was certain that . . . Perhaps she's remarried and changed her name. Let me describe her. Late fifties, gray hair, pink and white skin, a little plump . . ."

"Oh," the voice interrupted, sounding pleased to be clearing up a puzzle, "that sounds like Mrs. Lockett. But she isn't a guest here. She owns the Lilacs. She's at church now. Who shall I say called?"

Through a faint buzzing in his ears, Cosmo said, "John Rudd."

When Mrs. Lockett returned from the eleven o'clock service at St. Mary's of the Harbor, Mrs. Captiva, who always covered the office on Sunday mornings after going to early Mass herself, said, "A Mr. John Rudd called trying to reach—I think it was you, but there wasn't any message left."

"Rudd?" Mrs. Lockett's fine-skinned forehead wrinkled in thought. "I've never heard of him."

SIX

As always when the holiday season went into high gear with the Fourth of July, various jollities were in swing from end to end of the Cape, from Buzzard's Bay to Provincetown. There were regattas and clambakes, parades and parties, church bazaar cake-and-fudge fiestas, pony races on the beach, tennis, badminton and croquet matches, dune skiing and windsurfing contests.

And as always at this thronged and festive time, death visited the scene here and there. A drowning at the Coast Guard Beach in North Truro, three car accidents producing four fatalities, a man killed while motorcycling drunkenly through the woods near Barnstable.

On the Monday morning before the Fourth, the body of a windsurfer was found in the bay off Provincetown. An alarmed pilot of a power launch saw the body, well below the surface of the water, and radioed the police. The police launch retrieved the body, which was that of Ron McCallister. He was well known locally, a year-round resident who worked nine months of the year at Parr's Garage and three months during the summer at twice the salary as head cook at the Hickory Dickory Dock restaurant on Commercial Street.

The police launch, with the body on board, did a bit of searching and soon found what they were looking for: the smashed remains of a Windsurfer carried by the tide some distance from the drowned man. The gay little wreck, its purple-and-emerald-green-striped sails and mast floating on the water, told its own story. The sailboard was gouged almost in two near the center. It had obviously been struck broadside, and struck at speed, by a power boat.

The police, who were pretty well inured to trouble of this kind over the Fourth, were nevertheless puzzled. Why hadn't the power boat picked him up with it after it ran into him? And, then, McCallister was a swimmer, a good one, and wasn't all that far from shore, perhaps half a mile. Again, if it had happened at night, why hadn't the boat's lights picked up the brilliant sails in time to avoid a collision?

The autopsy placed the time of McCallister's death at a little after eleven on Sunday night. There was evidence of a blow on the side of his head, which was consistent with a laboratory examination of the near-split surfboard, which showed traces of blood in its splintered edges. It seemed clear that he had whacked his head when he fell.

There was no mystery about his going out on the water at night. He was skilled at the sport and often, after he had finished up at the Hickory Dickory Dock, could be seen boarding his craft. He had two of these, one at home and one that he kept in a shed on the beach behind the restaurant. There had been no moon, but there had been a tempting steady wind, and the lights from the shore vaguely illumined the water to some distance out. After that, night sight would take over for the lone, skimming man. Or at least it always had until now.

A police check on the bows of boats for any evidence of the collision was, in the words of one Sergeant Dutra, "at the least, impossible." There were thousands of boats up and down the Cape, and there was no reason to believe that the particular boat docked in Provincetown. Besides, a quick lick of paint after the boat returned to its mooring, wherever she was moored, would neatly erase the evidence.

On the local news at noon on Monday, a police request
was made that anyone who had been near the scene of the
accident and had heard or seen anything bearing on it to
contact them.

But the death of McCallister, to most people, including
the police, was another of those pointless, meaningless
wipeouts. The pilot probably drunk, his boat out of control. A hit-and-run case, only this time on salt water.

McCallister was unmarried, thirty-five years of age, living in a small second-floor apartment on Bradford Street.
He had no known enemies; he was a quiet man who kept
to himself. "If he was one of the boys, now," said a Sergeant Utrillo, "maybe it would be different. Sometimes
they get real mad at each other. But as far as anyone
knows, he wasn't."

"That McCallister who got himself torpedoed," Cosmo
said, "wasn't he a pal of yours, Buggie?"

He had walked over in his half-hour break time from
the Lightship to Buggie's apartment, if you could call it
that, at the end of Audley's Wharf.

"I knew him, yes. He'd come by for a beer now and
then. Too bad." There was nothing of heartfelt emotion in
Buggie's voice, but then there never was.

His proper name was George Eden. He had probably
been given the nickname in school because of his height,
or lack of it, a little under five feet. But he had other
undersized features—a small snub nose, a small folded-in
mouth. His face was round and freckled, his hair sun-
bleached and carelessly cut, obviously by himself, although it was said about him that he had pots of money.
His sharp dark eyes reminded Cosmo of cockroaches, the
way the brown circles flitted rapidly from left to right,
centered themselves, flickered about again as though on
watch duty on all sides at all times. He wore faded blue

jeans and a T-shirt that had seen better days, a dim gray with blue still showing at the seams. He could have been in his late thirties or mid forties, it was hard to tell.

His apartment reminded Cosmo of the one book of Charles Dickens he had ever read, he couldn't remember the name of it. The main room, where they sat now, had floors that tilted, crooked ceilings, and pockets of darkness, only one light on in the tarnished brass lamp on the table beside Buggie's sagging chair. Cobwebs veiled the corners. Noise and music came in the dirty half-open windows from the lesbian joint downstairs, called Sub Rosa's, said to be owned or partly owned by Buggie; although depending on whom you talked to he had a part interest in any number of local enterprises.

Buggie reached down and picked up a gin bottle from the floor. He poured a tot into a glass on the table, drank it, and said, "Well, there's to Ron, poor bastard. Care for a touch, Cosmo?"

"No thanks. I never drink raw spirits. You know, I always feel unusually good when I come by here, Buggie— handsome and well dressed, and it's all thanks to you."

"Each to his taste. Me, I like to be comfortable. And you've usually got another reason to feel good when you drop by. I won't keep you, I know you have to be back at the keys."

Cosmo watched him take a roll of bills out of his jeans pocket and count out well-worn fifties, twenties and tens. Then, carefully recounting the money handed to him, he put it in his slim leather billfold which became a fat leather billfold.

"Thanks," he said. "I'm off." The tilting broad-planked floor creaked as he stood up. "Some day this residence of yours is going to topple into the sea. Let's hope it's at low tide."

"Yes, my loss would be felt by many," Buggie said. "In ways, that is. Nighty-night, Cosmo."

His guest descended the dangerously flimsy old outside staircase and went up the cobbled wharf, past Sub Rosa's, a bicycle rental shop, a jewelry shop and a marine supplies store.

Buggie was reported to own the whole wharf. But nobody knew for sure.

Cosmo was waked at three by the guitar in the next room. He reached down in the dark, found a shoe by the bed and hurled it against the wall. Nothing happened. The guitar went on. It took a second shoe to silence it.

Trying to get back to sleep, he was caught up in one of those grim small-hours self-reviews that seldom strike by daylight. What was he all about, what was his life all about?

The sometime member of symphony orchestras banging away at a piano, hoping that tips would be sent his way instead of drinks, but a drink was cheaper and more often the offering.

An extra source of income, via Buggie, but a day-to-day dangerous one.

A loving Margaret in Nantucket starting to turn possessive; the next thing would be "Why don't we get married, Cosmo?" She was, he gathered, in moderately comfortable circumstances, but he was not devoted to moderation in his hopes of a better style of life for himself. The alliance would in any case wither on the stem when he went back to New York, or Florida, or somewhere to play his piano, at the end of the season.

He plumped up his pillow with a frustrated fist. After a while he slept through a blur of unpleasant dreams and woke sweating at ten, still under the spell of the last doomy dream. No—it was all right, here he was in his own room with the sunlight pouring in.

Going down the white-painted outside steps, he saw his landlady, Mrs. Oliva, sitting on the glider in the screened porch drinking coffee and reading *TV Guide.* She had, he knew, already taken somewhat of a fancy to him. He said through the screen, "Could you by any chance take pity on a hungry, thirsty man? All I need is a little coffee and a bit of bread and butter."

She patted the glider seat. "Come in and sit down, Mr. Toscanini. I'll go find something for you."

She was back in a few minutes with a cup of hot coffee, cream and sugar at the ready, and a large sugar-glistening Danish pastry studded with pecans. "This ought to keep body and soul together."

She was a dumpy little woman with the dark eyes of the Portuguese, now alight with interest and curiosity. "We haven't had a chance to visit, this is nice," watching him eat and drink. "Wasn't it awful, about that Ron McCallister? You probably didn't know him. He roomed here five or six years back. Are you going to the parade? You mustn't miss the parade, everybody goes, right down the end of this street is a good place to watch."

"No, angel of mercy, I did not know McCallister, but I feel for him. And of course I'm going to the parade. Will you accept me as your escort when the time rolls around?"

"Oh, yes indeed." She beamed.

Cosmo finished his breakfast and with the air of a man replete and content leaned back in the glider and lit a cigarette. He felt that now he could move obliquely to the matter that had drawn him to Mrs. Oliva's porch in the first place.

"I imagine you're a regular map and encyclopedia of this town," he said. "Maybe you can help me out. A friend of mine wanted me to pay his regards to someone he knows at a place called the Lilacs, an inn of some sort. He said it was at the end of town. Well, I walked all the way down—or up—to where Commercial Street joins Route 6A, and unless it's hidden in some lane . . ."

Mrs. Oliva's eyes sparkled at this opportunity to be helpful. "It's at the *other* end of town, you were going in the opposite direction," she said. "Oh yes, the Lilacs, everyone knows the Lilacs. Who's your friend's friend there?"

"A Mrs. . . ." he hesitated, "Pocket? Could that be it?"

Mrs. Oliva giggled. "No, but you're close. I think he means May Lockett. She's the owner since March."

As this was a subject Mrs. Oliva was obviously interested in, Cosmo felt no qualms in indulging further curiosity. "You mean she bought it in March?"

"No, she's worked there for twenty-five years or so for Miss Winthrop, as her assistant and sort of companion. It was a regular fairytale. When Miss Winthrop passed away she left the whole thing to Mrs. Lockett. You'll be able to imagine what it's worth when you head in the right direction and take a look at it."

"Well—but she and Mr. Lockett run it?"

"There is no Mr. Lockett, or, I seem to remember, I heard he died a while before she came up here. Some wondered she never remarried, not a bad-looking woman, but she didn't. She and Miss Winthrop were close friends, or as close as anyone could get to that woman. Nose in the air, fancy education, went off to Europe for a month every winter while Mrs. Lockett stayed home and took care of things. I don't do any winter business, but they're busy over Thanksgiving and Christmas."

"May," Cosmo murmured, almost as though to himself. And then more briskly, "May Lockett, not Pocket. Well, thanks to you, Mrs. Oliva, now I think I've got her straight."

SEVEN

In the afternoon, when the sidewalks packed for the parade were now back to their usual casual jam, Cosmo went to the office of a travel agent, unglamorously named Slattery's, two doors from the Caper. It was open, as he had expected; the season was too short and too precious for closing your business door to the crowds.

Only one of the three desks was occupied, by an attractive red-haired girl whose name on the desk plate was Amy Slattery. "Yes, can I help you with anything?"

"It sounds silly, I know," Cosmo said, "but sometimes you travel people can get reservations when the loner over the phone draws a blank. I want to stay at the Lilacs for a few days, preferably beginning tomorrow, while I'm here. I've heard it's a hard place to get into."

He had thought it unwise to address the owner-proprietor of the Lilacs over the telephone himself.

"We can but try," Amy Slattery said. "What's your name?"

"John Rudd. From New York." The name came to his mind without any effort at all.

He listened while she said, "Hello there, Mrs. Lockett, how are you this fine day?" (Good thing he hadn't taken the chance of making the call himself.) She asked about reservations and listened with a slight frown. She said, "Hang on a minute, I'll check that with Mr. Rudd." To Cosmo, "The inn is booked solid. There's a big suite of rooms across the street in a separate house, but also a part of the Lilacs, which would cost you one hundred and seventy-five dollars a day. It's being vacated as of tomorrow morning, and you could have it until checkout time on Friday, twelve o'clock. Do you think you . . . ?"

"It sounds fine," said Cosmo without turning a hair. "Yes, I'll take it."

"He'll take it," she said into the telephone. "Yes, John Rudd, New York. That's twelve tomorrow through twelve Friday. See you, Mrs. Lockett."

When she had hung up, Cosmo asked, "No deposit required?"

"No, the Lilacs still does things in a ladies-and-gentlemen sort of way and then, you're conveniently filling a time slot before the weekend rush starts again. You know where . . ."

She was interrupted by a young man bursting in at the door and crying, "Amy babydoll, you must, on pain of death if you don't, get me on a flying machine out of Logan for Los Angeles by noon tomorrow at the latest, the *very* latest." He was bare to the waist and wore tight giraffe-patterned jeans.

"Yes, I know where the Lilacs is, thank you," Cosmo said. The young man looked at him as he walked to the door. "Do I connect you with a piano? Well, that's beside the point. Los Angeles, Amy—get cracking."

As she began in an unruffled way tapping the buttons on her telephone, she said, "Yes, the Lightship. I imagine Cosmo is your professional name? Hello, Slattery's in Provincetown here, I want to book a . . ."

Cosmo terminated the semi-exchange by going out the door and closing it behind him. Did it matter if Amy Slattery had a one-time-only client who seemed to have two names? Probably not, in this town. Certainly not.

On Wednesday at noon he drove to the Lilacs through a chilly, heavy downpour. He did not give up his room at Mrs. Oliva's because he had no foreknowledge of which way his wind would blow.

One voice of his ego said to him, she might be enormously pleased to see her husband again. It was momentarily reassuring to toy with the idea that she had never taken up with another man because she had never met anyone to equal him. Had, over the years, bitterly regretted her flight—after all, married people did quarrel, and sometimes violently, but that was just a heavy wave breaking against solid surviving rock in many cases. But . . . she hadn't wanted to humble herself, say to him, "Will you take me back, dear Cosmo?"

Another voice, that of the seasoned adventurer and risk-taker, offered the opinion that she might reject him at the very threshold of the Lilacs, scream him away into the rain, or call the police. "There's a man trying to force his way in here under a false name. Will you send a patrol car immediately?"

He felt cold sweat under his shirt and his one good sports jacket, of pearl-buttoned ivory Shetland tweed. There was no getting around the business of registering in person and picking up his room key. Even if he had found someone else to do this for him, the disparity in appearance between the signer-in and the occupant of the suite of rooms would suggest dark doings to the most innocent eye.

Would a woman in control of this little empire, the Lilacs, feel it necessary to be chained to the front desk at all times? Hardly. Or, maybe.

Tossing in his bed the night before, he had gone over these ruminations many times. If, say, there was anyone else around in the lobby when he entered and she first saw him, he could burst into loud cries of joy and reunion. "My

darling May! . . ." and so on. She hadn't ever liked public
displays of emotion and might find it simpler and more
convenient to let him sign the card and hand him the key.
Face-saving, for her. She had been a businesswoman
when they married. She was still a businesswoman.

But if there was no one around in the lobby?

He parked his car in the sandy lot across the street, got
out his umbrella with an idea of using it as some sort of
shield or hiding place, opened the gate and went up the
path to the front door, which was solid, brass-knockered,
white-painted wood. Keeping his umbrella open, and
held so as to conceal his head and shoulders, he opened
the door and went in, to a room that bore no resemblance
to a lobby and was well filled with people, voices, laughter, warmth and firelight.

Standing just inside the door, he glanced to his left and
saw the office and the desk at which a woman sat, talking
on the telephone. The woman was not May. She was elderly and thin, with well-carved bones, sun-browned skin
and straight short iron-gray hair. A wave of weakness hit
Cosmo's knees and then passed. He lowered his umbrella
and walked into the office.

"John Rudd," he said. "Reservations for the . . . the
suite, isn't it?"

"Yes, right across the street, ground floor." She gave
him a registration card to sign. Fortunately, the card directed "please print," so there was no problem about
disguising his handwriting. "I remember your name, or I
connect it with the voice. Calling up a little while back
wanting Mrs. Lockett. She'll be back soon. She's visiting a
sick friend of hers in the hospital at Hyannis. I'll tell her
you're here, shall I?"

"No, don't, I want to surprise her."

She handed him a little ring with three keys on it. "One
for the house front door, one for your own front door on

the right in the hall, one for your back door in the kitchen. Mrs. Lockett likes people staying in the Winthrop suite to lock the house door when they expect to be out for a while, because her own apartment is on the second floor. And there's no one else in the house, so . . ."

"Yes, of course, I'll remember."

Cosmo lost no time in getting himself out of the office and through the sitting room under the interested gazes of the rainbound. *"She'll be back soon."* Behind the shield of his opened umbrella, he crossed to his car, got out his bag, went up the two-railed wooden steps of the clapboard house painted in the inn's washy lavender-blue, unlocked the door, and in the hall took a badly needed long, deep breath.

Suppose she had come back from Hyannis and come straight here? He stood for a few seconds listening to absolute silence, but silence was no promise of an empty house. Quickly, he unlocked the paneled white door on his right, went in and, without hearing himself, gave the released sigh of one who has after all walked the tightrope safely from one end to the other.

The living room was large and pleasant, with two sash windows looking out on the street and two French windows in the far wall, with a little terrace outside and willows clustering around a little pool. Cosmo crossed the green broadloom rug, lowered the blinds on the front windows to within eight inches of the sill, and pulled the cords of the floor-to-ceiling chintz curtains. The parking lot was on the opposite side of the house from the willow garden, but he pulled the curtains there too, and turned on lamps.

The door into the bedroom was open. He examined this attractive, comfortable room and pulled more blinds and closed more curtains. There were three doors, one to a large closet, one to the bathroom and the third to a well-equipped kitchen.

He unpacked his bag and put his few items of clothing in the closet and the top drawer of the bureau. Then he went back into the living room, having noted a fire neatly laid ready for the match, lit it, and sat down in a big graceful wing chair, upholstered in pale yellow silk damask and angled toward the hearth.

The fire began to burn merrily. The rain beat at the windows. An unaccustomed deep peace stole over Cosmo.

What, he asked himself, feeling a little unreal, was he doing here in what was undoubtedly the master suite at the Lilacs?

Looking over a new life to lead, was his first unthought-out, instinctive answer to himself.

And, to be more practical: to see and get the feel of the place, how successfully or not it was run, get a scent of its worth, and—and what?

To a man with a downhill future, the course was obvious. Grasp the main, the golden chance with both hands. Reunite with May, one way or another, take a lot of the burden of running the inn off her back, settle in for life as that glamorous and distinguished innkeeper, Cosmo Fane of the Lilacs.

What wonderful noises, crackling firewood and lashing rain . . . Cosmo's eyelids half dropped. He yawned and stretched in a kind of dream, of hope and contentment. He seemed to hear voices, enthusiastic voices. ". . . Rather a classy man, don't you think? Mrs. Lockett's very nice, but he does add a good deal to the place." ". . . You should have been in the sitting room last night when he played his cello for us. Concert quality, of course, he's played with all the great symphony orchestras here and abroad." "Have you heard that the Lilacs will be serving dinner beginning next month? That fabulous man cooked us a sample meal because it was my birthday, *Larousse Gastronomique* all the way, and the *wines . . .*" "Yes, and the bar's going in next week, I'm told."

Of course, a bar. Of course, a magnificent wine list. That's how and where the money really comes pouring in.

Perhaps rip out the broad stone terrace over the bay and have a swimming pool there, drinks served by the pool at lunchtime under great umbrellas. The umbrellas should, yes, be made of a lilac-flowered fabric.

Busy sociable profitable summers, bursts of extra business over the holidays, but otherwise quiet winters when perhaps they would go off south, he and May . . .

An end to the bitter singing for his supper—"Hey, piano man, how about giving us 'Hello Dolly.' " An end to the increasingly weary pursuit of Nutmegs in any town or city where he was trying to earn his bread. An end to having once been almost someone and now being nobody, a journeyman entertainer for people who mostly didn't listen through their alcohol. An end to the occasionally desperate, dangerous measures, like playing delivery man for Buggie's lightweight and enormously valuable cargo, carrying it in the cello case to Nantucket, to Hyannis, to Brewster and Dennis and Chatham and Barnstable.

His sleepy lids lifted a little. What, actually, had happened to Ron McCallister? Why his sudden and violent vanishing from the scene. He hadn't thought much about it until now, hadn't cared, possibly hadn't dared. McCallister had been, he was almost sure, working for Buggie on the side.

It would be, under all the circumstances, nothing short of madness not to try to make peace with May and move into the new life waiting for him here and now.

The sound of whistling came in through the front windows. There were brisk footsteps on the wooden stairs outside. Cosmo moved the drawn curtain and shade a little, and saw the military-looking man he had encountered at the gate of the Lilacs during his first surveillance. A moment later there was a smart double rap at his own door.

Let him in? Why not? It was time to stop playing the part of a prisoner, his own prisoner, in hiding here. He opened the door and the man standing there said, "Yardley. Thomas G. Yardley, U.S. Army, retired," as though answering some kind of roll call. "May I come in?"

Cosmo held the door wide to admit him and then closed it rapidly. "Good afternoon." He just remembered his name in time. "John Rudd."

Yardley was unbelting his dripping trenchcoat. "I thought it might be a nice idea to welcome a new guest with a noggin on a damned cold rainy afternoon." He took a silver flask from his pocket to illustrate.

Jesus Christ.

Was he the co-proprietor of the Lilacs, the other half of Mrs. Lockett?

He went to the kitchen and got glasses and ice, totally unable to think. Yardley followed him in and elucidated.

"I feel somewhat in the role of unofficial host because I've lived here myself year-round for eight years, in the west cottage." As they went back into the living room, he glanced appraisingly around. "Good setup you've got here. I still think of it as Miss Winthrop's rooms. Holy-of-holies kind of place, I've only been inside once or twice in all these years. Here, let me pour, my treat."

The two men sat down before the fire, Yardley in the other chair angled to it, a painted Boston rocker of ample size.

"Cheers. Are you planning a long stay here?" Cosmo, with his inborn wariness, read his mind. Fellow must be in the chips, the real chips, to spend one hundred and seventy-five dollars a day in the Winthrop suite. Possibly worth getting to know, this solid fellow.

"No, unfortunately, just a few days." He took a swallow of his scotch. What if Yardley came to dinner tonight, or any night, to the Lightship and discovered him playing the piano under another name? Okay—professional name. Maria Captiva, who might be cleaning his suite tomorrow, knew him by his own name. And he had given his first name to her brother, who also worked here.

"I seem to recall your face from somewhere—did you stay here, say, last month?"

"No, this is my first visit." Cosmo discovered that his glass had in some way emptied itself. The major noted this too, drank the rest of his, and poured a refill for both.

"Then you haven't met Mrs. Lockett, the, mmm, guiding spirit as well as the owner. Fine woman in her quiet way." He looked deeply into his drink and went on, "Rose blushing unseen and all that, matrimonially speaking. Odd she hasn't been snatched up before, but then of course until this year she was only, well, employed here . . ." Perhaps feeling this sounded a little calculating if not downright ungallant, "But a good cook, an even-tempered lady, pleasant disposition, I've never seen her out of temper. And quite a pretty color to her eyes and skin although I don't believe she smears stuff on to produce the effect." This last had an ominous, loverlike sound to Cosmo's appalled ears.

The knowledge struck him hard: that of course she'd be a prize, a comely woman taken to be a widow who had only a few months ago received an impressive inheritance.

"Hurry" was the word that came into his mind. Hurry. Hurry. The next week, the next day, might be too late.

Surely, if Yardley had secured her as wife-to-be he would announce it proudly? Maybe, maybe not. But even if it hadn't happened quite yet, catch a woman at just the right moment and you're in business, as Cosmo well knew.

Dropping Mrs. Lockett with something of the air of a man who has come a little too close to personal and private matters, Yardley turned to various wars, half wars, threatened wars and skirmishes going on here and there in the world, and explained to Cosmo just what mistakes were being made by all concerned and how he, Yardley, would correct them.

After finishing his second drink, he glanced at his watch. "Mustn't keep you, I'm due for a haircut," with a thoughtful study of Cosmo's richly growing hair and beard.

Ten minutes after he had left, Cosmo heard feet on the front steps, the door opening and closing. There was a short crisp knock on his door. Then May's voice, raised, firm, called, "Mr. Rudd?"

Cosmo sat very still in his wing chair.

Another call, a little louder, "Mr. John Rudd?"

He looked at his hands grasping the arm-ends of the chair.

There was a slight unexplained thump at floor level in the hall. Cosmo made himself get up and put his ear to the door. The stairway up was carpeted, he remembered, but he heard a creak or so and then the closing of a door above.

One of the maids?

If not, Mrs. Lockett had come home.

EIGHT

Old and solidly built as the house was, there were muted
overhead noises, a window being closed or opened, footsteps, and the thin faraway ringing of a telephone.

Cosmo took this last sound as the right moment to summon up his courage and see what had made the little
thumping sound outside his door. He opened it a foot or so
and saw a high-handled straw basket on the floor. Bringing it in, he found the basket contained a large bunch of
white grapes, a round wooden box of Brie, a package of
English water crackers, and a bottle of Inglenook rosé.
Attached to the handle with a little ribbon was a note in
what he recognized as May's handwriting. "Dear Mr.
Rudd, Herewith, the Lilacs' greetings to its guests in the
Winthrop suite. I hope you enjoy your stay with us. May
Lockett."

Five minutes after he had collected his guest basket, he
heard the door upstairs close, again a few squeaks of the
stair treads, and the front door closing. Had there been
someone else up there when May came home? He peered
through a twitched-back edge of the curtain and saw Mrs.
Fane/Lockett crossing the street under her umbrella, going through the gateway and up the path to the inn.

Entering her office to relieve Mrs. Captiva, Mrs. Lockett said, "Sorry I'm late, I stopped at home for a bite. Has
that man Rudd checked in?"

"Yes, a little after twelve."

"Is he all right?" The Lilacs did not vet its guests severely, only turning away those whose undesirability was immediately obvious to the eye.

Mrs. Captiva handed her his registration card. The printed address under his name was a number on East 63rd Street. "Yes, nicely dressed, well spoken, not young but not old either. He seemed a little nervous, but then people who arrive from New York City often seem that way, at first."

"I brought over his basket and knocked and then called his name but got no answer. Probably napping after the drive from New York, or did he have a car?"

"Yes. I went to look out the sitting room window to see if there was anyone with him, not registered, and he got his bag out of a black car. He was alone."

"Well, good. And thank you for being extra careful when it's someone staying in the house with me upstairs."

Cosmo's nature as well as his new perception about possible seekers for May's hand suggested that he proceed with speed.

Make it this evening. *If* she came home to dinner this evening.

He'd be late for work at the Lightship, but this would be the first time, and he was good at convincing excuses.

In his determined optimism—because pessimism he knew would be fatally crippling—he found no real reason to believe that she wouldn't at least half-welcome him, and indeed his reception might be a good deal warmer.

Most people as they grew older mellowed; a sudden flare of rage, or outrage, couldn't be sustained forever. Now, take him. He thought of himself with a touch of complacence as being a bit temperamental, which one would expect in a man of great talent. But things that would have infuriated him ten, even five, years ago he now took in stride.

Walking to the oval gilt-framed mirror to the right of the fireplace, he studied himself for a moment. All right, sixty years old. But look at Margaret Rudd, look at Mrs. Oliva, look at Maria Captiva sparkling at him.

Unable to sit down, he moved from room to room, working out the lines of what he saw as the first act of this domestic drama.

If that went well, and it might go marvelously well, the second act: dinner for two, just themselves, cooked by him for her, as in the happy early days of their marriage.

He picked up the telephone directory and found a grocery store that delivered. He said he was staying at the Lilacs, which for some reason seemed to be an open sesame with the grocery, Cudworth's, and that he would like to have his order delivered no later than five-thirty. Yes, sir, no problem, sir, what will you be requiring?

"Two shell steaks, choice ones, about an inch and a quarter thick. A bunch of asparagus if it's plump, I don't want the spindly kind. Three ripe tomatoes." No potatoes; May hadn't ever liked to eat them because she thought they were too fattening. "Breadsticks, if you've got the very thin ones, a pound of sweet butter, a box of red raspberries, and—do you carry liquor?" Yes, they did. "A bottle of good Beaujolais, and a bottle of kirsch for the raspberries. Fresh peaches if the raspberries are not perfectly ripe."

He felt happy, hopeful, and at peace, giving his order for dinner for two, a simple but delicious meal that wouldn't take much time to cook. They'd have so many things to talk about that that was the right plan. An ebullient thought struck him: what if the third, or rather fourth, act of the play was breakfast together? "A dozen eggs, a half pint of whipping cream, a half pound of lean Canadian bacon, a loaf of wholewheat bread, uncut if you have it, and coffee—do you grind yours freshly to order? Good. A pound of that."

The Cudworth's man thanked him and asked if he'd like to start a charge account with them. "Thanks, no, not at the moment." Paying in cash would be no problem; in fact he had far too much cash in his immediate possession for any prudent man to carry, most of it handed over by Buggie. He hadn't yet bothered to open a checking account in Provincetown. And he had long since ceased using credit cards; he knew from experience they were too easy to steal.

The afternoon stretched on and then telescoped. He showered and dressed in his best, dark-gray flannel trousers, the pongee shirt, still clean in this grime-free sea town, the ivory tweed jacket, a dark-gray knitted tie.

At the kitchen counter, he arranged some of the contents of his guest basket on a tole tray. He washed his grapes, took two wine glasses from the generously stocked cabinet, and two salad plates on which he would place his cheeses. Two knives, a corkscrew, and were there any napkins? Yes, paper, but large expensive paper napkins, white.

Wandering restlessly out of the kitchen, he saw something he hadn't noticed before, a little bowl of roses on the drop-leaf table between the French windows in the living room. Later, he would choose one pink rose to lay on the tray.

What if she didn't come home for dinner tonight? He would simply defer the whole process until tomorrow night.

But pray God she came tonight.

At five-fifteen Cudworth's delivered his order. Cosmo put his groceries away, examining each item in turn and unable to find fault with anything. Where would they dine, *if* they dined? Pull up the drop leaves on the window table and see. Yes, just the right size for two.

He badly wanted a drink from the bottle of scotch he had brought along but hesitated; it might reach her nose.

At ten minutes of six, the front door opened and closed, and a moment later the door at the top of the stairs closed.

What if she was just coming home to change, on her way out somewhere? He prepared his tray in haste, forgetting to add the pink rose. He went out into the hall and up the stairs. There was a long mirror on the landing where the stairs right-angled. He saw himself with his tray.

Christ, he thought, I look like a waiter.

He gave a light double-knock on her door. "Yes?" her voice called from quite near the door. He had no choice but silence. Let her think it was perhaps someone looking for John Rudd on the wrong floor.

He heard the sliding of a bolt. The door opened. He moved with a neat swiftness past her and put his festive little tray on her coffee table. Turning, he said, "Good evening to my long-lost love."

There was no entrance hallway; the door opened directly into the lamplit, comfortable room. Near the door was a tall, slender walnut bookcase filled with paperbacks, and beside the bookcase was a straight chair with the seat cushion embroidered in needlepoint. Very slowly, she sat down on this chair, hands braced against the cushion edges.

Talk, not fast, but in a rich heavy flow so that he would not be easy to interrupt until he got to his point, or points. Waving toward the tray, he began, "I thought I'd like to share my gifts with the giver. To think, May, of all the years we've been separated, and me thinking, my God, is she poor, is she alone, is she ill, does she need help, just

because one afternoon I lost my temper and threw away
my life, my whole life?"

He waited a portion of a second. She was looking at him,
her eyes wide, and blank. There was absolutely no expression on her face, the mouth not quite firm but curving
neither up nor down.

"I passed by the Lilacs a few days back and the miracle
happened. There you were in the doorway, looking well,
and pink, and safe, and looking *May*—life obviously
hadn't given you the battering it's given me, and I was so
happy, there was the bluebird I thought I'd lost sight of
forever."

Silence. He heard the rain against the closed windows.
Was there a slight stiffening about her arms, her hands
gripping the cushion?

He had acquired over the years stage presence, professional confidence. The thing to do was to press on deter-
minedly, even against the feeling that the audience had
left the theater in a body.

The thought went through his mind that what he was
seeing before him—and of course not hearing at all—was
the state of shock. In such a state, each word, each phrase,
would take a while to sink in. Was, she might be thinking,
was he real, this man standing six feet away from her, or
was it all a dream?

Put it into words. Help her out. "Don't you think, my
darling, a glass of wine would help?"

She neither shook her head nor said a word but continued staring, like—like what? Like one of those creatures,
squirrels and things, who froze, hoping the hunter or the
enemy wouldn't know they were there at all.

To show his own ease and command of himself, and his
sense of truly belonging here, with her, he opened the
bottle of rosé, poured himself a glass, and lifted it to her.

Were her cheeks beginning to tremble slightly or was

that just a passing nervous spasm? Was she going to faint? It would be no bad thing in a way if she did. He could lift her tenderly, carry her to the sofa, watch beside her with close, loving eyes until her lashes lifted.

What if she had a tricky heart and was on the brink of an attack?

Get on with it, he ordered himself. Get to the point.

"I thought what an incredible blessing to find you, after all these years, *now*. You look as delightful as ever, but you're not a young woman, May, and this inn is an immense burden for you to carry alone. When we're together, as a man and his wife should be, I can lift at least two thirds of the burden off your shoulders. I can assure you I'm entirely well and strong after what I described as the battering life began to give me after you . . . you left me. I suppose I began not really giving much of a damn then, I felt so lost, or to put it even more strongly, so bereaved. My idea, which I think couldn't be more practical—as well as bringing with it a great deal of joy—is to work in tandem as"—no harm in repeating it—"husband and wife. I could even offer our guests, in addition to everything else, entertainment of a very high order, piano or cello, it does give a place an air like nothing else."

Now her lips were beginning to shake a little.

"And think of the winters, repairs, heavy work, painting and carpentering, landscaping, I'd take over for all your different odd-job men, I like hard work in the winter air and I've always been good with my hands. People like husband-and-wife teams, you know, at hotels and inns—it makes the place homier, more personal. And with your own work more than cut in half, we might be able to drift somewhere south in late winter . . ."

He found he had run out of breath and out of his basic material. He poured wine into the second glass and took three firm steps toward her. "Come, can't we toast our new and happy and *second* future?"

A powerful surge of adrenalin gave her the strength to rise to her feet, but she still held onto the corner of the chair back. With a gesture she had never before resorted to, she took the glass from his hand and threw the wine in his face.

He had no handkerchief, fresh or otherwise, with him and had to wipe his cheeks and forehead with the palms of his hands.

"Oh, well, now, May, of course you're surprised and upset . . . shock does funny things but . . ." This came out in a hoarse gasp. Averting his eyes from hers, which he found unbearable to look into, he glanced down at the pink splashes on his ivory tweed lapels and brushed at them with his fingers.

Her voice was slow and cold, and contained. "Everything you have said to me in this room is hereby erased, gone, forgotten, never spoken and never listened to. With perhaps one exception—that life *has* given you a battering, because unless it had, you, even you, wouldn't come on hands and knees, begging for your bread and water. Or was it attempting to threaten, for your bread and water?"

Now it was his turn to be silent. Now it was his eyes that were fixed, stunned, on her face.

"I would call the police and have you evicted instantly, but I don't want commotion here, guests wondering about sirens, and a man struggling in handcuffs being dragged away, very likely shouting and swearing at the top of his lungs. Or crying, over his spilt milk? Possibly. You have reservations for one more day here and will of course vacate at or before checkout time at noon on Friday."

She paused for a moment, in the icy assembling of her

next words. "Although if I were in your position I shouldn't like to waste another one hundred and seventy-five dollars to attain the total of exactly zero. And now, goodnight and goodbye, Mr. Rudd, which you choose to call yourself, and just as well—because, for me, no man of your own name really exists at all."

She walked to the door and held it open. He left straight-backed and not lingering. Now it was he who had to fight back the tears of shock. And of rage and devastating humiliation.

No man of your name, Cosmo Fane, really exists at all.

NINE

It took Cosmo twice as long as it should to pack his bag. His mental and physical coordination was awry. He would stop in the center of the bedroom on the way to get out the scanty contents of the top drawer of the bureau and wonder why he was moving in this direction, what it was he was supposed to be doing next.

At one point he discovered himself sitting in the wing chair, bent forward, hands clasped loosely between his knees.

He felt heavy and clumsy, like a man made of stone.

Drawer emptied. What next? The jeans and sweater from the closet, sneakers from the closet floor, put them in the bag. His umbrella. His raincoat. Into the bathroom, for toothpaste and toothbrush, was there anything else of his in here? Medicine cabinet shining-clean, holding nothing on its shelves. Holding nothing of Cosmo Fane's.

The groceries in the refrigerator never crossed his mind. He put on the raincoat, picked up his bag, and went out of his Winthrop suite, not even glancing in the mirror as he went past it. He had no desire to see his face.

Mrs. Lockett watched, from above. She had switched off all but one lamp and knelt on the floor at the window, looking out from under the bottom of the shade, which was drawn to within an inch of the sill.

She had been at this post since he walked down the stairs. In a little over fifteen minutes, she saw him going down the front steps, carrying his bag and his umbrella, the rain falling on his bare head.

Her eyes followed him across the street and into the inn. The office had no window looking out on the street but he must be in the office now, handing in his keys, paying his bill. "Sorry," he would be saying to Dominic who was at present doing office duty, "I have to leave, something urgent has come up."

Motionless, she kept her kneeling position even though it was getting a little painful. He came out and down the path, crossed to the parking lot and drove away, headlights on. The rain and low clouds made the evening very dark.

She went to the telephone and sat thinking for a minute or so before she made the call. The remotest hint of any connection between her and the departed guest was absolutely out of the question. Not only for simply personal motives of pride, of position; but for reasons she had yet to sort out and perhaps never would.

"Dominic? I saw the Rudd man going out of here with his bag and I wondered what that was all about? I thought he was booked through Thursday."

She glanced at her windows; as usual when she came home she drew the curtains for privacy after her public day at the inn. No one could have seen even the shadow of a man standing in this room.

"He checked out a few minutes ago, paid the full sum, no attempt to bargain, and just said he had to leave—no reasons given. He looked . . ." Dominic hesitated a second, but he was an articulate young man, "clenched, his face, his whole body, the way a fist is clenched. Or as though he was holding himself together, to put it in another way, and just about managing. His face was a funny dark red, but with no expression on it at all. He gave me a

sort of jolt, as though I'd touched a faulty electric connection and handed myself a shock."

"Oh well, as we know, it takes all kinds," Mrs. Lockett
said, having to force her normal placidity into her voice.

"But there's something else that's funny, that I—sorry, I
have to cut off, people coming to check in, I may call you
back."

After handling his registering, Dominic sat thinking.
He had the liveliest interest in the human race; he was a
writer and a natural gobbler of material. After his gradua-
tion from Amherst, to which he had gotten a scholarship,
he began writing, while working at the inn in summers
and in winters working for a friend who was a painter and
carpenter. He had sold several short stories, one to *Play-
boy* and one to *Ellery Queen's Mystery Magazine,* and was
midway through a novel about the fishermen of Provincetown. His father had been a fishing captain before his
death in a northeaster on the Grand Banks. His working
title was "The Blessing of the Fleet."

This man, now. This clenched man. He had gotten an
impression too, which he hadn't passed along—perhaps it
was overactive imagination—that the man in some way
resembled a bomb that would be going off any minute
now. You could almost sense the ticking.

He picked up the telephone and called his home on
Snow Street. After a short wait, Maria answered and then
hearing his voice said, "The shower's turned on, make it
fast, Dom, I was about to step in."

"That dark man with a beard who stopped by here a
while back and asked for you, named Cosmo. Cosmo
What, and where was he playing the piano when he met
you?"

"Why?"

"I'll tell you later, this office is jumping now—just one
minute, Mrs. Tracy, and I'll be with you—"

"Cosmo Fane. He plays the piano at the Lightship." Today had been her day off. She asked with interest, "Did he come around wanting me again?"

"Not exactly. Go take your shower."

Next he called Mrs. Lockett. "I don't know if you'd be interested, but this same man stopped by while I was working in the garden a week or so ago. He wanted to, uh, have a chat with Maria, and I told him she was busy. That time he gave his name as Cosmo. When I told her about him I think I said he looked to me like a bad-news man. She says he plays the piano at the Lightship. Whole name there is Cosmo Fane."

The telephone surely couldn't pick up the thud of a heavily beating heart?

Mrs. Lockett after a pause suggesting consideration of a minor matter, said, "There may be some perfectly innocent explanation, but . . ." She lowered the pitch of her voice, too high, sounding unlike her even to her own ears. "We don't want mystery men at the inn, not in this day and age, do we? While you think about it, Dominic, and before I forget, you might just put him in the red folder, at least for the time being. I don't like the idea of two names. Especially in terms of credit cards and personal checks and so on."

The red folder contained a slim flat file, alphabetically tabbed, which contained the names, addresses and brief descriptions of guests who in one way or another had earned a blacklisting while staying at the inn. This file was automatically checked when anyone unfamiliar called for reservations. There were not a great many names in it.

Dominic's favorite offender was a wealthy middle-aged man who was discovered rambling naked along the terrace in the moonlight at eleven o'clock one night; he explained that he had a habit of walking in his sleep.

On a sheet of paper from a small pad, he typed the two

names, the description, the New York address, and the place and nature of employment at this date.

The collapse of Cosmo's aerial empire got him to the Lightship to work on time, after all. On this rainy evening the restaurant was only half full, but people were still arriving. Chunky driftwood logs burned in the great stone fireplace at the far end of the bar, sending a ballet dance of flames, mauve, green, pale blue, about and above the heart of orange and red.

He had been tempted to say the hell with it, the hell with everything, and skip the piano tonight. But, dumping his bag in his room at Mrs. Oliva's, he resisted the temptation, of which he himself would be the only victim.

Sitting at the elderly but well-tuned Baldwin upright, he wondered at first if his fingers would work, or instead just lie still and limp on the keys.

One of two women sitting at a nearby table called over, "Can you play some things from *The King and I?* We just saw the revival. I'd almost forgotten that marvelous music."

Cosmo started with "Whistle a Happy Tune." His fingers did work. As he played on through the score, he felt a little wave of returning confidence at least of the performing flesh and bone. He could sense the pleasure and gaiety his music was kindling, all around the room.

Of course, go on with this job. He'd need it, at least for a while, until something could be worked out.

Forget the whole thing? Settle for Buggie, for Nutmeg and her ilk, for playing songs to drink with and eat lobster to? Never.

People could be played on, like instruments.

His spirits began to rise at the sounds he was making, here at his piano. "Hello, young lovers . . . I've been in love like you." She'd been in love. She might think it over and be swept with regret, remorse. She might call him tomorrow or the next day with some kind of proposal.

Cosmo, I'm sorry I was so hasty, it was just the suddenness, the shock, I said a great many things I didn't mean at all . . .

A great many things. Until this minute, he hadn't been able to face calling up one word of what she had said. ". . . *you, even you, wouldn't come on hands and knees begging for bread and water.*"

The brief, mild exhilaration produced solely by his music vanished. An almost overpowering red rage filled the vacuum, the annihilation she had left deep in the center of his being.

Ten minutes later, the hostess, Claudine, came over to tell him that the couple eating lobster three tables to his left wanted to buy him a drink. "Your usual scotch?" She touched his shoulder and bent her head close to his, her silver-blonde hair swinging against his cheek. "My, Cosmo," she murmured, "you're sure setting that piano on fire tonight."

At two o'clock in the morning, Mrs. Lockett woke with a start and without immediately knowing why sat up straight and tense in bed, braced on one arm. She had taken one of her prescription sleeping tablets, which she only felt the need for once or twice a year. When, at ten o'clock, she had tipped the capsule out of the bottle, she had hesitated a little before swallowing it.

After all, he was gone, checked out, the house locked up. Then why, combined with a heavy fatigue, the result of somehow managing an outward calm and control while he was standing there, why the acute, boiling nervousness all through her body? It was that conflict the pill would have to handle, or tired as she was she wouldn't sleep.

Now she heard what had probably brought her wide

awake and upright. The rain had stopped but the wind had risen, tossing the branches of the willow against the window glass. Or was that what had waked her? Had she been dreaming, something important, something vital?

Downstairs. There hadn't been a sound downstairs, had there, in the rooms that to her were still full of Cosmo's presence? No, of course not, old houses built of wood had night noises of their own, wind noises, frost noises in winter.

She found herself thinking of all sorts of terrifying possibilities, downstairs, where he had been.

She thought of a pile of oil-soaked rags lying on the floor under a window deliberately left an inch open, and a lighted match being tossed in.

She thought of keys taken to the hardware store—after all, he had had the keys in his possession for six hours or so —and copied, so that he would have his own permanent set of keys to this house. Silent feet perhaps even now coming up the stairs. Would her bolt hold against a heavy savage shoulder?

Because, of course, he would be savage, after what he had said and what she had answered to his outrageous proposals. He wouldn't just go away sighing and shaking his head over what he might have considered a promising try gone down the drain.

What might he do about it?

What might he do to her, about it? Tonight, or tomorrow, or next week or next month.

Before she had gone to bed, she had forced herself to go down the stairs, unlock the door of the suite and, standing just inside the doorway, make the briefest inspection. Yes, the lights were all out, empty and total darkness facing her, not even a glimmer from the street because all the curtains were drawn. The darkness frightened her. She hadn't wanted to explore further. He was gone. If there was any Cosmo clutter left behind him, Susan and Maria would tidy it away in the morning and then he would be really gone, his presence wholly erased.

Going down there again at this hour, checking again, was unthinkable. And from another point of view irrational. Mad.

She should have asked Dominic, nice reliable Dominic, to sleep on the sofa in her sitting room. But how could she possibly have explained the request? "That man Rudd, I was afraid he might come back and . . ." Dominic would think with good reason that the capable Mrs. Lockett, who had always been able to cope with any crisis little or large, was now turning dithery, poor thing.

As a rule not a highly imaginative woman, she saw herself alone, totally alone, on a bare, level, treeless plain where there was nowhere to hide, with Cosmo standing facing her. There was no one who could help her.

No one but herself.

A belated physical reaction hit her. Nausea, and a swimming head. Grasping at the wall to hold her up, she got to the bathroom just in time and was violently ill. Stomach muscles sore, water running from her eyes, she went trembling back to bed.

She closed her eyes and deep-breathed to stop the trembling. Sleep was probably impossible, but one had to try. One had to be strong.

Oh, I could kill him, she thought, looking down a long dark corridor with no glimpse, at the end of it, of the sunlight of a vanished peace and serenity. Oh, I could kill him.

TEN

Seeing Susan Perry crossing the road in the morning sunlight with her cleaning cart, Dominic abandoned for the moment his staking of delphiniums in the border, caught up with her, and said, "Let me take your cart, Susan, it's too much for a fragile southerner."

Susan gave him one of her blue looks from her tilted eyes and said, "I am quite able to take care of myself in every way, thank you, Dominic."

Three or four days after her arrival at the Lilacs, she had been selected by Dominic, at least on his part, for his own. A sure and solid feeling, no question whatever about it.

Not a man to linger when he had an object, he began almost at once, affectionate, teasing, close, as if they had always known each other and always been more than fond of each other.

He drew a polite blank. After a while he said to his sister, "Susan, what about her? Is she all tied up with someone down south or here?"

Maria grinned at him, having observed the proceedings. "You mean you can't understand how anyone can resist *you?* Actually, I'll tell you a secret, Dom, she told me she'd had her heart broken on her early in spring, February or March, terrible time of the year to have a broken heart I think, and that she was going to hold still, those were the words, for quite a while. She said that after making such a bad mistake—I gather the man ran off with her best friend—she was not going to jump into any more traps until she was older and her judgment was better."

"How much older, did she say?"

"She didn't specify. She runs with my group, when she does go out to play, but nothing, you know, happens in the male department."

"Oh well," Dominic said with his cheerful vividness, "hope does, occasionally, spring eternal. I'll just press on."

Now, appropriating her cart with one swift strong gesture, he said, "As a matter of fact I have an ulterior motive. I want to go in with you and look over the suite."

"For what?"

"I want to see if there are any dead bodies in closets or any forgotten weapon stashed away in a drawer." Susan hadn't heard about Cosmo, anything about Cosmo since Maria's enthusiasms on the first day she came to work. Dominic told her about him, and about his arrival and unexpected departure. He also introduced his other, unspoken reaction to the man checking out. "He felt to me like a bomb about to go off."

Susan looked alarmed and hesitated before unlocking the door of the suite. "You don't mean to say you think he might have left some sort of explosive inside, here? I do feel people are very casual with their bombs these days."

"I'll go in first and take a quick look around. You wait here."

Over his shoulder, he added, "Bear in mind that if I get blown to bits you will have lost your own, and only, true love."

He saw that Susan would have very little work to do, cleaning up the suite. Three cigarette butts in one ashtray, the dead fire to be cleared away. The bed hadn't been slept in or even napped on. His accompanying Susan here had been merely an excuse to be at her side, but underneath he still felt a strong curiosity about the recent occupant.

"Okay, free and clear as far as I can see," he called from the kitchen. Joining him, Susan said, "You have given me the feeling that somehow I am walking into a haunted house." She opened the refrigerator door to see if there was anything inside to be cleared out. "Oh, my."

Onto the counter came the steaks and asparagus and fruit and cream and all the rest of the projected dinner and breakfast makings, and a bottle of Beaujolais. "Heavens, what am I to do with all this? Should I . . . ?"

"It's yours," Dominic said. "Finders keepers as far as left-behind food goes, that's the rule of the inn. But you wouldn't have found this feast if I hadn't made it possible for you to enter without danger, so we'll call it ours."

"But your man, your strange man, might remember and come back for it."

"No go, he's checked out and food can't be left to spoil and molder, unsanitary." He began opening packages. "I'll tell you what. We'll have dinner on the beach, grill the steaks over a nice fire. Ma can cook the asparagus and we'll eat that cold. Come to think of it, it does look like dinner for two. Maybe that's why he left so suddenly, disappointed in love—like so many of us. She just plain didn't show up."

"Dominic." Susan's tone was severe. "I fail to see why you cannot speak one sentence, or paragraph, without putting the word love in it."

Leaning against the counter, arms crossed on his chest, he smiled seraphically on her. "I had an idea the other night. Suppose we think of ourselves as chums, or brother and sister. That way we could see all we wanted of each other without making it any problem for you."

Susan took a red raspberry and nibbled it. Still severe, "You already have a sister." Was that faint dent near one corner of her mouth a suggestion of a smile, or was it just the nibbling?

"She's not my type, although a nice girl in her way. Seven o'clock on the beach then. The tide will be dead low." He left abruptly without waiting for a possible refusal.

Susan thought it was strange that, after he had gone, the air still seemed to vibrate with his presence. She had had that feeling before.

She went home at four to her rented room and bath on Parasol Street, napped because she had been up until three the night before with Maria's assorted group, and then, comfortably yawning, dressed. Nothing too fetching. White cotton pants, blue and white gingham shirt, white sandals. With the mental reminder that, as she had told Dominic, she was quite able to take care of herself in every way, she bicycled to the Lilacs for the dinner picnic with her newly acquired brother.

Near the foot of the steps from the terrace where the sand was warm and dry, he was busy building his fire. A plastic laundry basket he had brought held everything that would be needed, from wine glasses to steak knives to a jar of dip for the cold asparagus. "Ma's own mayonnaise, lemon and garlic and tarragon. Made fresh this afternoon for a bullying son."

While the steaks on the hand grill were sending forth enticing scents and sizzles, Susan raised her glass and said, "Well, here's to Mr. Rudd or Mr. Fane or both, for this Lucullan repast."

"I like the elaborate way you talk, only it sounds natural, from you—or is that getting too personal for our new footing?" He watched with pleasure as she hungrily cut into her smoking grill-striped steak. "Anyway, I had an idea about our host. Let's, no rush about it, wander into the Lightship later for a drink. They frown on it during dinner hours, but the hostess is a friend of mine, so no problem."

Susan thought about telling him she had a date later, but relented upon dipping a stalk of asparagus into Mrs. Captiva's delectable mayonnaise. "Your object being to case the man, as they say?"

"Yes. In the flesh, at the piano, to see if he's as much a fake in that department as he is as a guest."

It was with a delicious sense of daring and adventure, as well as a slight nervous fluttering somewhere under her ribs, that Margaret Rudd embarked on her journey from Nantucket to Provincetown on that Thursday afternoon.

What fun, to take Cosmo by surprise.

She took the midafternoon ferry, driving her car aboard and then leaving it parked below at water level to climb to the main deck. Bringing the car was expensive, but she didn't want to be at the mercy of bus schedules if things didn't exactly . . . She left that thought dangling.

She had no clear ideas, in fact, about this visit, which had occurred to her in the small hours of this morning, when she was feeling lonely in her big empty bed. Well, simplify it: she had never heard him playing the piano. It would be great fun to see and hear him performing, see how his audience liked him, and it would be fun too, to slip quietly in and have him discover her in some candlelit corner later on. Rather a nice compliment, to come all this way to hear him play.

She had in the past paid several visits to the Lightship with her husband, and mentally chose a table well behind the piano. That is, if the layout was still the same, the piano facing away from the entrance door toward the bay, placed in the center of the large ell-shaped room.

Reaching Provincetown at a little after seven-thirty, she parked her car in a garage on Bradford Street and walked down through Lovett's Court to Commercial Street. She wanted it to be a little darker when she went in. The late light was still glowing brilliantly off the calm water of the bay. Of course, he started work at seven, so there would be no chance of his seeing her now, strolling idly along the street, looking in shop windows, stopping to buy a pair of enameled pink hoop earrings. Trying on the earrings in the shop in front of a mirror, she thought she looked quite nice in her gray silk bow-tied blouse, accordion-pleated white skirt and black linen box jacket; the early July evenings could still produce chilly breezes. She took off her white earrings and put on the new pink ones, which went exactly with the color of her lipstick.

Stroll another ten minutes. Why was the nervous rib-fluttering still there? Why did the word "furtive" cross her mind, a word she had never thought of in connection with herself?

After all, she wasn't here to spy on him, catch him off his guard (and these thoughts were new too, or at least until this moment unspoken in her head). She was here to give them both a surprise, a treat, the unexpected things were the most fun of all.

Fortunately, a group of five people were going in at the heavy planked door when at eight-ten she walked up the stone pathway through its gay little garden to the restaurant entrance. The hostess seated the group at a table evidently reserved by the front windows over the water and then came back to where Margaret was standing.

Yes, the piano was still in the same place, Cosmo's back was to her. Yes, the tables were each lit with candles stuffed into wax-dripping bottles, so there were helpful pockets of deep shadow.

"Table for one?" the hostess asked with a slight lack of enthusiasm in her voice, the prospect of a hefty check and lavish drink ordering being dim in such a case.

"I'm being joined a little later, but I won't wait. I'll order a cocktail," Margaret said firmly. Not exactly an untruth. Of course, Cosmo would join her later. The musicians usually got break time, or to put it more gracefully, intermissions.

A waitress arrived at her table, which happened to be just the one she had wanted. "A Manhattan, please." As she was near the fireplace end of the bar, the drink arrived quickly. She sat sipping it while she watched Cosmo and heard what struck her as his masterful playing. Such confidence. Such power. That was *her* Cosmo, filling the room with music.

The hostess, who was slender, young and very pretty, went to sit on the bench beside him. She bent toward him as if to whisper something into his ear, her hand casually lifted to lie on his shoulder.

Take your hand off his shoulder, Margaret said silently, savagely.

She was probably just repeating a request or so from diners for songs they'd like to hear. And naturally they'd be, Cosmo and the girl, friends, associates, seeing each other every night, working together. Younger people were often free and open with their gestures of affection, which often meant nothing at all.

Two tables away from her, Dominic said to Susan, "Well, whatever else he is, he's one hell of a pianist. Seems a funny thing he's content to play to the clatter of crockery and the chomping of jaws."

When Claudine got up off the piano bench, Dominic beckoned to her. He introduced Susan and then asked, "Your man at the piano—Cosmo Fane, is that his name?— isn't he almost too good for the likes of the Lightship?"

"Cosmo's great, isn't he," Claudine agreed. "He played with symphonies, but his health took a bad turn and he

decided on the resort life, at least for a while, salt and sun
and all that."

"He looks in remarkably good shape now. Let's hope
you don't lose him to a Philharmonic somewhere."

Noting the close attention being directed at them from
the nearby table, Claudine went over and asked, "Everything all right? Would you like coffee with or after your
dinner?"

"After, please," Margaret said, her voice forbiddingly
cold. Streak of the bitch there, Claudine thought. She
found her job an excellent training ground for the study of
humanity.

Cosmo finished playing Cole Porter's "Night and Day"
and right after the last note a man, one of a party of four
next to Margaret, shouted inaccurately and a little drunkenly, "Hey, fella, how about 'Hello, Mame?' "

Cosmo turned his head, looked at the man, then looked
at Margaret. She felt herself flushing and smiled at him,
raising her eyebrows as if to say, Fancy meeting you here.

Cosmo had to fight to conceal a rush of astonished rage.
What was she doing, sneaking in here unannounced,
watching him from her shadowy corner flickering with
candlelight? Why no previous telephone call from Nantucket, or why no note via Claudine to tell him she was
here?

There was nothing for it but to go over to her. Passing
the party of four, he said, "I'm due to return to the piano
in half an hour," and sat down with his back to them,
across the table from Margaret.

"This is a surprise, to say the least," he began, his voice
low. For a moment, and for some unidentifiable reason,
Margaret was frightened of him.

"That's what it was meant to be," she said, short of
breath and rushing on, "I wanted to hear you play and

you're marvelous, fabulous, I'm impressed out of my
mind, not only the cello but the . . . And I meant it to be
a surprise, is it a nice one?"

Margaret's waitress put down before her her plate of
steak and French fried potatoes. "Careful, plate's hot. Another Manhattan, or maybe a nice cold bottle of beer?"
Margaret shook her head and the waitress said to Cosmo,
"Bring you a drink, doll?"

"No thanks," Cosmo said. "Don't let your dinner get
cold, Margaret . . ." She noticed that he had no com-
ment one way or another about the surprise.

To fill the little silence, she murmured, "I thought that
perhaps after you finished playing we could, well . . ."
Spend the rest of our night together, Cosmo, a sort of pre-
reunion before the weekend.

Under no circumstances would he allow her to see his
shabby poor-man's room. Forgetting that he had used the
same excuse before, he said, "I'm booked to play at a party
out near Race Point, probably, damn my luck, pretty well
all night."

"You do a lot of that, don't you." Flat voice. Then he did
remember.

"My dear Margaret." He laid his hand on hers. "Embar-
rassing as it is to admit, I have to pick up what I can to put
some kind of living together."

"Yes, it's not like Nantucket, is it? Where you really
don't have to pay for anything." Her color was high.

Don't dump Nantucket, don't let the anger show until
the other arrangement was assured, the Lilacs arrangement.

"Of course the last ferry's long since gone. Maybe Claudine can help dig you up a motel room . . ."

Claudine at this appropriate moment brought him a
folded note. He glanced at it, frowned, and said, "I have to
leave you for a few moments. Don't run off, when I come

back I'll play all your favorite songs, I know your list by heart. What delightful earrings, are they new? I'll see you in no time."

"All right, I'll wait." Only a little sour trace of the sulks left. "I suppose I can stay with friends in Wellfleet. It's lucky I brought my car over."

The note from Buggie said, "Drop around now in your break time, something's come up."

A clear, male voice said, "Good evening, Mr. Rudd. Nice listening to you." He looked to his right and saw young Captiva, who had checked him out of the Lilacs the night before. He nodded to him. All taken care of, the name, or would be when needed: the business of a professional name.

With the tide still low, Cosmo went out through the kitchen, took a shortcut along the beach to Audley's Wharf and climbed the rickety stairs. He knocked, opened the door to Buggie's mutter from inside, and said, "Where to?—the delivery."

"Well, that's a question, isn't it," Buggie answered from the depths of his sagging chair. There was a deliberate insolence in his voice. "Whether you're safe enough for me any more. Or whether . . ."

He paused and looked hard at Cosmo. Without his summoning it up, a picture came into Cosmo's mind, a little wrecked Windsurfer, a body, dead, floating under water.

Nonsense. One of Buggie's gambits. It was Margaret's unnerving appearance that had thrown him off balance. Suspicion everywhere, no safety, no dignity left.

"What the hell do you mean?"

"What the hell do *you* mean—moving just like that out of the Oliva dump and into the ten-dollar-a-minute bridal suite or whatever it is at the Lilacs. Don't you know there are eyes in this town watching and waiting to see people throwing around piles of new money? Eyes in uniforms and eyes in plain suits? And you just a wayside piano player, who travels about to private parties at rich people's houses and commutes to Nantucket on weekends with a cello case . . ."

He let his voice trail off. He poured himself an inch of gin and looked browsingly into his glass. He had Cosmo on a small but very hot rack and wanted to see how he would get off it.

If Buggie ever got his hands on a whisper of the story, what would he do about it? Something, there was no doubt about that. Something big, something Buggie. Blackmail to start with, perhaps.

Thinking hard, Cosmo tried to buy a few seconds of time. "Am I to assume your mighty organization"—allowing himself a smile—"has me followed night and day?"

"No, someone saw you checking in, carrying your bag in, this is a small town, remember."

For the second time in half an hour, Cosmo had to humble himself. "There's a girl there, you know her, Maria . . . If you must know, I wanted her to get a different picture of me. Man who could afford a suite just for the pleasure of being near her and all that . . . Not just piano-banging Cosmo but a man of means in an imported English tweed jacket . . ."

Buggie obviously didn't know he had checked out six hours after he had checked in or he would have been catechized on that too.

"You romantic musical types," Buggie said. "New world to me, I must say." He didn't look entirely satisfied, but the ugly look had gone away from somewhere behind his cockroach-scuttling dark eyes. "Well, stick to your dump and if you make a few tips buy yourself another English jacket."

Cosmo, with no further word to speak and no ability to

do so without, finally, letting go of his temper, left the room and went down the steps.

In a way it was dismaying that Buggie had of necessity been told that there was even the slenderest of threads tying him to the Lilacs.

ELEVEN

According to Cosmo's mental timetable, if May was going to change her mind and accept his offer of help, supporting strength—partnership—she would probably change it no later than Friday or Saturday.

Just a guess, of course, and he admitted to himself that it was probably calculated more on the basis of his own impatience than any knowledge of who she was, now, what she would do now, and when.

He swept aside the words "if ever."

On Friday morning, before he left Mrs. Oliva's, he accepted her invitation to a cup of coffee on the porch and said he was expecting an important phone call. There were no telephones in the bedrooms, just a pay phone in the hall, very much in use most of the time, with young men in drooping attitudes whispering or laughing or scolding into it. He rather doubted that she would call him, anyway; a note would be more like her. Or, more like the way she used to be.

Mrs. Oliva promised that she would listen extra hard for any ringing and would instruct her daughter Effie, who made up the other half of the staff of Bayview Lodge, to do the same.

Strolling along Commercial Street, with the idea in mind of a refreshing Bloody Mary around eleven o'clock, he wondered for a moment if Margaret might be somewhere behind him, Margaret on monitor duty. But she had said, when he went back to the Lightship after his break, that she had called her friends in Wellfleet, would stay there for the night, and would see him on Saturday.

She had looked mollified, in fact beaming, when on his return he announced mysteriously and romantically through the hand microphone, "I am now going to play a very special medley for a very special lady, let's call her Madame X."

Thinking about Margaret, who would be waiting, head on her pillow, for the murmured, "And now, dearest Nutmeg . . ." brought suddenly into his head what struck him as a blinding revelation.

May had—of course she had—expected that their reunion would be accompanied by a renewal of marriage relationships.

She no doubt saw him as he was, still a strongly sexed man, and after all the quiet years of keeping herself to herself, would back away in near-maidenly terror from an invader in her bed. Why hadn't he thought of this glaringly obvious reaction before? It explained with perfect total clarity her total rejection of him.

A *physical* rejection, no more, no less.

He was astounded that until this moment he hadn't spotted the real truth, the real barrier. It was a minor matter to him, he couldn't care less about playing lover to a woman of her type and age. But she had no way of knowing that. Looking back, he remembered how often, and deliberately, he had repeated the words "husband and wife." He had meant to emphasize that there was still a solid legal tie between them, but she had (as he saw again her shaking cheeks and heard her icy voice) entirely misread his meaning.

Well, get about setting her straight, and right away.

A practiced hand at ordering flowers when the necessity for such a gesture arose, Cosmo went into the Windflower Shoppe. A boy of eighteen or nineteen was stand-

ing in front of the counter saying, "Yes, I think that's it—
the largest and ugliest cactus you have in the place, in fact
the ugliest I've ever seen. Just what I wanted. Gift-wrap it,
please, large green ribbon bow on top if you have a nice
color of poison green."

Cosmo half-heard the woman behind the counter protesting that it was a lovely cactus, some people loved and
even collected them, and it should produce a greenish-
yellow blossom or so in several weeks. He himself was
studying the glass case of flowers.

White carnations, suggesting purity. With maybe a
spray or so of innocent baby's breath. No, too much like a
bridal bouquet, the wrong thing altogether.

". . . I want it delivered as soon as possible to a Mr.
Wilbur Jennings at the Anchors Aweigh. I've written this
note, please tuck it in under the ribbon." It was not hard
to imagine the general tenor of the note. The customer
went out, smiling to himself.

Something safe, neutral, and without memories, Cosmo
thought. Gladioli ought to do it. One dozen of the peach
color and one dozen of the pale yellow. "While you're
wrapping these I'll write a note."

The note on the small stiff white card presented difficul-
ties. Be straightforward, that was the best thing. "My dear
May, As, in your quite natural surprise, our conversation
was cut short, I hadn't the time to assure you that it is
taken for granted our relationship as we work together
will be entirely platonic." For a few seconds he hesitated.
Did that smack of, Who wants you, you old bag? But there
was no other way to put it. Put it firmly and clearly. "In
addition, thinking back, there were a number of other"—
he reached for another card, his handwriting being of
large, bold style—"practical matters I had intended to
discuss with you, among them the business of our two
names, and will be looking forward to doing so in the

immediate future. Be assured I have good workable answers for everything. Yours, Cosmo."

Having addressed the card's envelope and paid for his flowers, there was nothing to do now but wait. But surely, the long white box delivered, the note read and mused over . . . surely the major stumbling block was removed, now and forever.

He had his Bloody Mary, and at one o'clock a porch lunch to which he had been invited last night by Claudine. "Cosmo food," she had said, and produced smoked salmon with capers, bakery-bought but delicate rolls to spread with paté, lemon ice trickled with rum, and more run in the demitasses. After lunch she gave him the impression of being more than ready to retire with him into the bedroom, but Cosmo was too restless. There might be a telephone message waiting for him. Or a note dispatched.

"I'm expecting an important call, marvelous lunch, see you tonight," and all Claudine got for her pains and her expense was a swift warm kiss.

When he returned to Mrs. Oliva's at four, she called, "Flowers came for you, Mr. Stokowski. I had them put in your room."

The box looked familiar, but then most florists' boxes look alike. He opened the box, peeled back the pale, waxy, green tissue, and found his sheaf of gladioli. It had been lifted out, scissored twice through the stems, and then placed back more or less together, grim mutilated flowers. There was no note.

No sensible or able woman, Mrs. Lockett informed herself, is subject to being pushed into a corner in this day and age.

In spite of this firm stance, underneath there was the

feeling of being caught in a terrible trap, the jaws of it not quite locked together but inexorably closing.

She sat by her window having a late, six o'clock cup of tea. A storm was approaching in heavy smoke-purple from the west, distant thunder rocking the air. You couldn't stop a thunderstorm advancing and breaking over the town, over the Lilacs, no matter how sensible and able you were.

Her glance lit on a peach-colored gladiola bud on the table, which had been overlooked when with shaking hands she had repacked the sheared sheaf of flowers. She picked it up and threw it into the wastebasket beside her chair.

What alternatives did she have for the overhead explosion of her personal thunderstorm?

She thought it would be madness to try to buy him off. Here is five thousand dollars, and for this sum it is understood that from now on you will leave me alone.

He would inevitably be back for more after he had spent it, having discovered that the rewards for a hands-off policy were there for the asking.

She could hardly go to the police and complain that a man she had once been married to was making a nuisance of himself, and would they please charge him with something or other? There had been no physical threat, no violence of any sort on his part. Not yet.

She was unaware of her forefinger lightly touching the place where his blow had split her upper lip.

Keep on rejecting, refusing, hold firm, deny his existence? Instinctively she knew this would increase, for him, the challenge.

Institute proceedings for a very much belated divorce? On what grounds? She had left him, deserted was the legal phrase, not he her. "And did you report your husband's attack on you to the police at the time? Wife abuse is pretty solid grounds for divorce these days." No. No, I didn't report it to the police.

Let him spread talk, spew revengeful gossip about her all over town? My own wife, Mrs. Lockett of the Lilacs. Only she isn't Mrs. Lockett, she's Mrs. Cosmo Fane.

If the whole story came out, it could hurt the Lilacs badly, niceness being one of the main things its patrons liked about the inn.

At noon today, she had been sitting on the terrace having a mild gin-and-tonic with Mrs. Nye. The three-year-old Nye twins, their hair white-gold, their skins a delicious biscuit-apricot color, were sitting close by, dangling their legs over the edge of the terrace. Thomas Nye, their father, came bounding up the stairs out of the summer sea. He was a New York investment banker.

"God, I haven't felt this marvelous since my first swim here last summer," he said, reaching for his own waiting gin-and-tonic. "Congratulations, Mrs. Lockett, for keeping everything right on target, so much the same. We think of this as one of the last nice places left anywhere."

Mrs. Nye and the boys, with their nurse, stayed at the Lilacs every summer for one month and then went on to spend August with his mother at Boothbay Harbor. Thomas Nye flew up in his private plane every weekend.

Nice, that was the best word of all for the Lilacs in every way. Nice big bedrooms with nice fresh calico-patterned wallpaper. Nice absence of swaggering swimming-pool types, to say nothing of the eternal conventions and conferences going on at big hotels. Nice help, mannerly and obliging. Nice guests, many of them who were now, after years, old friends of each other. Presiding over it all, nice Mrs. Lockett.

The rude realities of the contemporary world pushed nicely, safely aside, for a week, or two, or in several instances the whole lazy summer.

And now, over the invaluable niceness, the special quality of the Lilacs, fell the great shadow of a man.

("Have you heard the news? I still can't quite believe it. Mrs. Lockett has been married, secretly, for years and years, to the man who plays the piano at the Lightship. And her last name isn't Lockett at all!")

She took a final sip of her tea, which was now cold. Had she been wise to go asking for some possible immediate retaliation by destroying his flowers and sending them back? Instead of just placing them, impersonally, in a vase in the inn sitting room?

To have accepted his flowers would surely have sent him a message. I, Mrs. Lockett, accept you, Cosmo.

And by implication accepted everything his note stated and implied. ". . . our relationship as we work together . . . practical matters I had intended to discuss with you . . . will be looking forward to doing so in the immediate future."

As long as there was a Cosmo, her life, her present and her future, were not her own any more. They were, very dangerously, in his hands.

Staring straight into the literal truth of the word "unbearable," Mrs. Lockett deliberately turned off her mind. She got up, washed and dried her teacup and saucer, and went over to her office to pay bills and to write a nice cheerful letter to her friend Lucy Ellis in the hospital at Hyannis. It was so pleasant to get chatty letters when you were flat on your back in the hospital.

TWELVE

Without thinking at length about it, any more than deciding whether to brush her teeth after meals, Mrs. Lockett started on her preliminary explorations Saturday morning in the kitchen at the Lilacs.

As always when the inn was fully occupied, she took a hand with the preparing and cooking of breakfasts. She was frying bacon at the stove, while at her side Mrs. Captiva scrambled eggs in one pan and kept an eye on her poached eggs in another at the back. Maria was toasting English muffins and cinnamon-raisin bread and pouring glasses of fresh orange or cranberry juice.

Mrs. Lockett lifted out of her pan eight strips of delicately browned bacon and put them on paper toweling to drain. She said, "A friend of mine is planning a party for her daughter and was very much impressed with the man playing the piano at the Lightship. She wonders if and when he is available."

"Oh, Cosmo," Maria said. "He plays there five nights a week, not just now and then, so . . ."

"At what hours? Perhaps before his night work starts—would that be rather late?"

"No, seven till two."

"And what about weekends?"

Maria had, earlier in the week, urged her friend Eddie into a second expensive dinner and evening at the Lightship and had had another téte-a-téte with Cosmo—well, almost, if you left out Eddie sitting there, who didn't seem to enjoy the performer's visits to their table.

"He goes over to Nantucket and plays in the Admiralty in the evenings, a cello I think he said, in a string quartet or something like that."

"Maybe for an extra fee—for the party, I mean—he could arrange a night off. Have you an address or phone number where he could be gotten in touch with?"

"He said he lives in a dump on Lisbon Lane. I don't know the exact address, but he did give me a phone number."

"Maria," said her mother more or less automatically, "you don't want to take up with any of these New York people who turn up here for a couple of months and then walk off."

"Having an interesting conversation with a—a musician is hardly what can be called taking up, Ma," Maria said. "I've got the number somewhere in my bag here, if I can find it . . ." She wrote the number on a torn-off corner of a breakfast menu card thrown into the trash because it had a small grease spot on it, and handed the scrap to Mrs. Lockett. "I wouldn't mind doing him a good turn. He played 'Maria'—He said it was from some famous musical called *West Side Story*—just for me."

Mrs. Lockett went back with placid efficiency to her bacon frying.

Last night's storm had not done what thunderstorms are confidently supposed to do, clear the weather with a series of hammer blows and leave a cool sparkling in their wake. It was a damp, dark morning, the air so full of moisture it looked and felt like a first cousin to a fog.

Mrs. Lockett tied over her head an enveloping triangle-folded dark blue silk scarf, put on dark glasses, got into her car, locked all the doors from inside, and drove to Lisbon Lane.

It was not one of Provincetown's quainter and more colorful streets. The houses were small and shabby, built close together. There was a general sense of discarded domestic equipment lying about rusting in yards, and of thin cats wandering. It was to Mrs. Lockett a rather unfamiliar passageway between Bradford and Commercial, not a short route anyone would take by deliberate choice.

A little more than halfway down Lisbon Lane, she saw Mrs. Oliva's Bayview Lodge, with bicycles leaning against the unkempt hedge and a dingy-looking towel, on which reposed shiny brief red bathing trunks, hanging out of a window.

Across the street and one house down, Mrs. Braga lived. Mrs. Braga had worked for twelve years as a maid at the Lilacs before her arthritis caught up with her and forced her to retire.

Seeing, in the dim morning, lights on in Mrs. Braga's little clapboard house painted pea-green, Mrs. Lockett went past, to Gilman's Bakery on Commercial. She bought half a dozen of Gilman's justly popular breakfast buns, made with nutmeg and hazelnuts and filled in the center with apricot preserves. She drove back to Mrs. Braga's, turned into the grass-grown driveway, and parked her car behind the house beside an antique refrigerator lying on its side. She knocked at the back door, which as she remembered opened into the kitchen, and Mrs. Braga, a heavy handsome woman in her late fifties, answered it.

"How nice to see you on this gloomy old morning, Mrs. Lockett! More of this and the season will turn sour on us, won't it? But I suppose the Lilacs is full, God bless it."

"I just thought I'd drop by to see how you are. I've only had a cup of tea. Will you join me in coffee and buns? Gilman's."

"Now, that's cheerful. I've just made fresh coffee, I'll heat the buns for a few minutes."

These refreshments were served on a tray in Mrs. Braga's immaculate little front room, where the two sat on a cretonne-covered sofa facing the street from the opposite wall.

After a leisurely exchange about the Lilacs, which Mrs. Braga considered as a form of beloved alma mater, Mrs. Lockett said, "I'd forgotten that big rooming house—well, it's called a lodge, but still—was across the street from you. Is it very noisy? Does it bother you, summers?"

"Yes and no. You know the P-town types, and she gets mostly the lowest of the low. Fights and shouts, people—men—throwing messages and flowers and things into other people's—men's—windows at all hours. Craziest getups this year you ever saw in your life, a regular show. Yesterday I saw a boy in a sarong, nothing else but, oh yes, a seashell tied around his ear."

Mrs. Braga paused for breath and an appreciative bite at the apricot center of her bun. "Thank God my bedroom's at the back so that I don't get the whole of the night commotions, but there's one fellow who plays the cello, always very late, nasty sad groaning sound like ghosts walking around except most ghosts don't make any noise. I don't know why she puts up with it, but I think she may have an eye for him. Showy, foreign sort of looks, beard, if you like that kind of thing. I've seen her giving him breakfast on her porch, and she's not one to hand out anything for nothing."

"Well, but he's just there for a few days I suppose, maybe soon you can sleep the night through . . ."

"No." Mrs. Braga gestured toward the outside stairway going up to the second floor of the Lodge. "He's been there for, oh, more than two weeks. Goes off weekends with his instrument case but always comes back Mondays.

Someone told me, I don't know who, that he plays the piano at some restaurant or club here. Whenever anyone checks out she always hangs up her for-rent sign, ugly old orange neon-looking thing, and there's been not a glimpse of it. I think his room is the one right off the outside landing at the top of the stairs, sometimes his curtains aren't quite closed . . . I've never seen anyone else, male *or* female, in there with him."

A woman forced to idleness with nothing to do but watch television and her neighbors, Mrs. Lockett thought, could be a terrible trial, but in this case a blessing.

Mrs. Braga halted abruptly. "Here I've been running on, I'm ashamed of myself, but it's so good to see you and of course there aren't many people on this street I enjoy talking to, after those nice people . . . all those years . . . always such nice people."

"I've enjoyed every minute of it," Mrs. Lockett said, rising from the sofa. "Take care of yourself, Joanna."

THIRTEEN

"Good evening, Mr. Rudd."

Margaret had been turning it over in her mind for several days, dismissing it, coming obsessively back to it. She had probably misheard the young man saluting Cosmo. The party at the table next to hers, one of whom was that silly drunken man who had shouted to Cosmo, "Play 'Hello, Mame,'" had been very noisy.

She hadn't had a chance that evening to ask Cosmo about it. There were too many people around, and she didn't want to approach him at the piano and sit down and whisper to him as Claudine had. And it was getting on for ten o'clock, it wouldn't do to arrive rudely late at her friends' house in Wellfleet.

But if she hadn't misheard, was it some sort of flattery, of secret possession, his using her name?

It couldn't be a cover-up name to hide him from a pursuing wife. Some time back, she had asked him timidly about his marital past and he had said, one marriage followed by divorce, twelve years ago, and that he'd just as soon not linger on the subject if she didn't mind.

She thought now and then that she saw a faint, far glow at the end of the season, at what would have been parting time for them: that after the happy comfortable summer he would ask her, in his own colorful off-hand way, to marry him.

On the ferry going over on Saturday, Cosmo himself remembered "Good evening, Mr. Rudd." Well, probably Margaret hadn't heard it.

But it would be a bit tricky if he had to explain the matter to her. He gave a few moments of thought to this problem as, drinking a bottle of beer, he sat on the main deck of the ferry and looked out at the uninviting steel-gray water over which showers shook themselves out of the low clouds every ten minutes or so.

She picked him up in the Buick at the ferry dock, looking remarkably well, younger, in a rose-colored pantsuit and her new pink earrings. Cosmo reflected to himself, Well, no matter what anyone says about me, I'm good for women. Saves them paying out a fortune to get their skin massaged and creamed.

"On this nasty day, we'll light a fire to warm you up even if you have to dash off so soon," she said, turning into her sandy driveway. Not a word so far about Mr. Rudd, what a relief, surely she would have asked the question right away, women being the creatures they were, unable to contain urgent curiosities?

He dressed in the formal evening black-and-white she liked so much, and came out to join her in a glass of the usual chilled champagne she had on hand for his evening send-offs. The radio was on softly, Dvořák's Eighth Symphony. Eyes half-closed, she sat evidencing pleasure in the music, and sighed a little. "Isn't my fire nice? And the —whatever it is they're playing . . . Cosmo dear, maybe I'm crazy, but I could have sworn that young man a couple of tables away said to you when you passed him, after you got that note, 'Good evening, Mr. Rudd,' and some nice compliment about your playing."

Cosmo frowned slightly and took a thoughtful sip of his champagne, giving every appearance of one casting back mentally to pick up some minor matter. Then he smiled.

"Oh. And yes, it was a compliment. There's an English pianist, Ambrose Rudd, young but already beginning to make his mark internationally. I believe he's only appeared a few times in this country, but he's made several albums of records." Let it go at that; he had learned long since never to embroider a fiction.

She felt for a moment flattened and a little disappointed. He put out a hand to hers, lifted it, and kissed it. "Though I must say it's nice to share your name in public like that, in a perfectly legitimate way."

On Sunday, the weather was brilliantly clear, but it turned out to be somewhat of an unlucky day for Cosmo.

He and Margaret slept late, breakfasted on the little front porch with its tubs of scarlet geraniums, and then Margaret suggested they drive to Jetties Beach for a swim.

Cosmo had never learned to swim and disliked the idea of appearing in any inept light. "You shall swim and in the European fashion I shall bathe," he said. "Salt water, which with most people clears the sinuses, murders mine."

He owned no bathing trunks, and she got, from a closet in the garage containing her husband's clothes ("Somehow I never could bear to dispose of them, you know what a silly sentimental Nutmeg I am"), a pair of his trunks, conservatively cut black cotton. Giggling as he appeared in them, she said, "They're too big in the waist. Here, I'll lend you one of my stretch belts, the water won't hurt it."

Cosmo endured rather than enjoyed the three-quarters of an hour at Jetties Beach, sunning himself against a dune while Margaret busily breast-stroked back and forth thirty or forty feet out. He did take one cautious dip because his skin turned from agreeably to uncomfortably stinging-hot; immersing himself to the shoulders, splashing the water into foam with his arms to indicate vigorous action of some sort. Margaret, annoyingly, swam close to watch him having his European bathe.

"Someday, when you're more at leisure, I'll teach you to swim . . . Mr. Rudd," she said.

Was this to become a standing joke, a just-between-us, possessive intimacy?

It could get out of hand. It was already, in fact, out of hand: her "someday" complacently anticipated a long, shared future.

To restore himself to his position of unquestioned superiority in all matters worldly, in everything that really counted, he said when they got back to the cottage, "Don't jump into a shirt and shorts, my girl, I'm taking you to lunch at Totter's Tavern."

Totter's was a Nantucket institution, very old, very expensive, a crooked two-story house dating from the 1820s, deep in its English gardens, overlooking the Sound near Brant Point Light.

Margaret was thrilled. "In all these years, I've never even *been* there, I've always heard it was so grand. But I suppose, to you . . ."

Reservations on a dazzling Sunday in early July could have been a problem but the violinist in the Admiralty string quartet was one of the bartenders at Totter's by day. "Mention my name whenever you have trouble getting a table. My uncle's the maitre d'."

They were given a table by a window in the sought-after upstairs room. Margaret, glancing around wide-eyed, said, "There's Roger Mudd, I've always liked Roger Mudd, and I suppose that's his wife with him? And isn't that man in the corner Karl Lagersfeld?—I've seen his picture in Vogue, he designs the Chanel clothes now. And . . ."

"And across the table from you is a distinguished musician," Cosmo said with a smile. "Shall we live dangerously and have martinis?"

"Just one for me, they're apt to go to my head . . ." A little nervous among these glistening people, she picked up the menu, looked it over and said in a scandalized way, "Even the fish is outrageous, and they catch it right here!" But she looked happy and excited. Or did for ten minutes, until the tawny-haired girl carrying a gin-and-tonic came over to the table. She wore a pale blue man's shirt with the tails tied around her waist and Roman-striped silk pants. Her shirt buttons were undone, every one of them.

She had obviously had several drinks but wore them well. Her eyes seemed to reflect, sparkling, the blue of the Sound beyond the window. "Don't tell me, I know," she cried in an uncaring wealthy voice unafraid of listeners. "Dmitri, divine Dmitri, that's who you are. Who played the violin at the Admiralty that night and then we all went off and God, what a party." She cast an uninterested eye at Margaret, who looked a little white around the nostrils.

"Cosmo," Cosmo said calmly. "And it was the cello. I'd introduce you but I'm afraid I don't remember your name either."

"Oh, don't bother, I just rushed over to say hello, couldn't resist it." She bent and ran her fingers through his beard. "I'd know you in the dark, though, from the feel of that beard. So nice and crisp and silky. Well, I must get back, come play for me and play with me soon." Turning, she added, "Elizabeth Bigham, I'm in the book."

The waiter appearing at his side, Cosmo took this opportunity to turn off the heat for the moment. He ordered bluefish and a baked stuffed tomato for Margaret, and Welsh rarebit and Molson's ale for himself. "Are you sure," he asked Margaret, "you won't have the entrecôte? I know how you love steak."

"Certain, thank you. I won't empty your wallet any more than I can when you have to spend so much time after hours playing for . . . for private people. Was that the night when you had to go on playing, till quite late, at a private party at the Admiralty? Yes, it must have been, it was the only night you got home so terribly late. When I was so worried about whether something had happened to you."

During lunch, which was very good, he managed for the time being to smooth her over somewhat, explaining that as a performer you met all sorts of people and couldn't very well do anything about it.

With mock indignation, he said, "Surely you wouldn't want an audience spitting on a performance of mine, hissing and booing, complaining to the management that this poor oaf has five thumbs on each hand?"

"No, of course not, but . . ." Outwardly, she let it drop. Inwardly, she thought, The way she ran her fingers through his beard, and said how it felt . . . He must at least have been kissing her, or worse, a lot worse . . .

It was another of Cosmo's misfortunes that day that as he and Margaret emerged from the doorway of Totter's and were turning left, to go through the arbor of pink and white roses to the parking lot, Margaret's friend Jean Latimer, in her old tan Ford Pinto, passed by on the road.

Jean, who also rented out a room or several every summer, had fared badly in that line this season, having accepted as her boarders a young woman who turned out to be hopelessly untidy, unmarried as well, with two terrible children of three and five years old.

And here was Margaret being wined and dined by that, well, not young but extraordinary-looking boarder of hers. Margaret, who had abandoned her pretty little flowered shirtwaist dresses and sensible plain white sneakers for new and what Jean called showoff clothes. Margaret, who had been looking suspiciously younger, glowing, since sometime in June.

Jean got home to find that Montagu and Ashley, respectively the boy and the girl who infested her blue-and-white painted house, had scribbled all over the front door with their mother's scarlet nail polish. A great deal of it had dripped onto the little brick porch, and into the clay pots of lobelias.

Oh God, why did this have to happen to *her*, while Margaret . . . She managed to contain herself until after dinner, having grimly commanded the children's mother, Alida, to see to the mess in front. Then from the kitchen came the sound of a dish smashing on the floor; Ashley had not liked her dessert of Indian pudding.

At eight-thirty, feeling a sort of verbal vomit rising in her throat, she gave Margaret a ring. After an exchange of how-are-yous, she said, "I happened to be passing by Totter's and saw you with your roomer, did you treat or did he?"

"Oh, he did, of course."

"He's a very festive man, isn't he? Knows how to enjoy himself wherever he is."

Margaret didn't quite like the sound of that. "What do you mean? I mean, in particular?"

Jean described with zest (she was already beginning to feel much better) seeing Cosmo in Provincetown on Friday, around one o'clock. She had gone there to visit her sister.

"Well, Ellie's house is on Parasol Street, and right smack across the street, on the second-floor porch, there was a party of two. Very romantic setting, grapevines and hanging baskets full of fuchsias, he lounging on a chaise, and Ellie said the girl was the hostess at the Lightship, very pretty I must say. Ellie remarked to me—they've been a bit pinched since Joe got laid up and can't work—'It gives you a pain sometimes to see how the other half lives.' Lunch, wine and all, something pink that looked to me like smoked salmon, the girl just, pun intended, *barely* dressed. Ellie's chairman of one of her Congregational Church committees and worries anyway about the things that go on in summer in Provincetown, but I say—don't you?—if you can have a little fun, grab it, life's short. After their dessert and coffee they disappeared inside, so of course for us the show was over . . ."

"I'm sorry, I must stop talking, I think I hear my strawberry jam boiling over," Margaret said in an odd high voice.

She had almost four hours to wait to go and pick up Cosmo, four hours to sit, simmer, and several times, like her mythical jam, boil over.

The girl coming to their table at Totter's—any fool could tell that he hadn't been playing at a late party that night, but had spent the time with her, when she had acquainted herself so intimately with the texture of his beard. And Claudine beside him on the piano bench, whispering, touching, Claudine entertaining him to lunch for two, when she had comforted herself by deciding they were just working associates. ". . . they disappeared inside, so of course for us the show was over . . ."

And she, Margaret, giving him his room, or rather her room, and herself, free, handed over.

At eleven she called the Admiralty and left a message for him: she would be unable to pick him up in her car tonight.

Let him take a taxi instead of having the faithful, unquestioning—blind—Margaret at his beck and call.

She felt a frightening building up, as the time went by, of the pressure of rage, as though she was going to burst.

But she couldn't go to bed, feeling like this. She had to let the pressure out or it would drive her mad.

She saw his taxi stop in front of the cottage at twelve-twenty. She was sitting stony-eyed on the sofa when he unlocked the door and came in.

"Something wrong with the car?" he asked. "Or, I thought perhaps you weren't well, I was worried . . ."

He went to the tray on top of the low bookshelves where, since his advent, she kept a bottle of scotch and several glasses. Tonight there was no ice in the silver bucket. He poured one drink and was starting to pour the second when something in the air, a dark chill, reached him.

"Nothing for me," she said. "And I'm well enough, I suppose, except I've been sitting here thinking about all sorts of things, about you."

"Such as what?" Cosmo asked, unprepared, astonished, although, thinking back, that girl's appearance at the table at Totter's had been unfortunate to say the least.

In her accumulation of fury, she swung an axe instead of selecting a rapier.

"One of the things I was thinking about was that it's funny, no matter what you say, my being named Rudd and being . . . connected with you, and another pianist named Rudd. Are you sure you're not using my name in Provincetown to sign checks or something? Or get credit? Or borrow money, or something?"

There was a short, bad silence. "I mean, living off women the way you obviously do," she said, another brutally explicit swing of the axe.

As what was to him the only alternative to striking her, he flung his glass hard into the fireplace. Crystal bits and powder exploded back onto the rug.

He got his bag from the closet shelf in the guestroom and going past her into their bedroom packed it, while she sat motionless, exhausted and no longer able to think at all. He went to the telephone and called a taxi. "As soon as possible, please, an emergency."

He went out the front door. Behind him, the lock clicked. Five minutes later she saw the taxi's headlights as it stopped in front.

Now, it was all right. Now, she could cry. But it wasn't so much crying as a sort of howling, no one to hear it but herself, and through the open windows the silent moors.

FOURTEEN

Cosmo went in his taxi to the ground-floor apartment of a house on Wimple Street where Herb Devereaux, the violinist-bartender, lived. Seeing a light still on in the living room, he knocked at the door. "Mixup in Sunday night reservations," he explained to Herb. "Can you fix me up for the night?"

"Sure, if the couch will do. I'd invite you to share the bedroom but my wife isn't the type for a threesome." He brought a pillow, sheets and a blanket, provided a generous nightcap, and disappeared into the bedroom.

Cosmo spent a good deal of the night awake. He figured in the morning that all in all he had gotten at the most two hours of sleep.

Not wasted hours, though, he thought, going over on the morning ferry. He hadn't just been lying there, he had been thinking with all his wits. And if the night-conceived plans seemed a bit surrealistic by day, well, you always felt a little off-center, a little unreal yourself, without even a halfway decent sleep.

He picked up his car in the parking lot and got into Provincetown at a little after twelve. It was, thank God, sunny. Rain would complicate everything. He walked down the cobbled lane to Pepe's Wharf Restaurant, considered by many the very best in town. He wanted drink and good food, rest and comfort. And he wanted what might be called a witness of sorts.

The restaurant occupied a handsomely restored two-story clapboard house by the water, with a widow's-walk roof deck on top. Its founder and owner was Arne Lund, who had until his early retirement been a highly paid art director in a large New York advertising agency. Pepe's Wharf showed Arne's impeccable spare Swedish taste throughout, elegantly simple waxed birch tables and chairs, silver and crystal of the best and the plainest, uncurtained floor-to-ceiling windows offering the bay and the beach as additional decor.

Not many people here yet. Good, he'd get a chance for a chat with Arne. The two men met casually, now and then, in bars, and as fellow New Yorkers fell into an easy comfortable acquaintanceship.

Bar first, Cosmo thought. It was a pleasant, ample bar, with deep cushiony banquettes on three sides covered in silvery-beige wide-wale corduroy. When he went in, its only occupant besides the bartender was a large white cat sitting on a bar stool lapping milk from a saucer on the bar.

He ordered a martini, knowing it would be made with one of the best and most powerful English gins. A long, badly needed swallow emptied half his glass. Three people came in and settled themselves on the banquette, talking and laughing and calling to the cat. Karen also came in, Arne's daughter, an attractive worldly blonde with Garbo cheekbones; she managed the bar and was the restaurant hostess. She nodded to Cosmo, with a wide white smile. They too were casual street-meeting acquaintances who had had an occasional drink together, but she had never shown any signs of being carried away by his charms.

She stood at the open end of the bar, the wall telephone right behind her head, scanning the scene to see that everything was all right, down to the last bowl of smoked salted almonds.

Cosmo, who was near her end of the bar, finished his drink, ordered another, and said, "Do me a favor, Karen, since you're right by the phone? A friend of mine wants the suite at the Lilacs tonight, will you see if it's free?"

She made the call, laughed a little into the telephone, turned and said, "No, occupied. I got Maria. She says it's a very old lady staying there for a week. Afraid someone is trying to poison her, and is a vegetarian into the bargain. She brought along a tremendous box of celery and carrots from some health store and Maria says the vegetable bins in both their refrigerators as well as her own are jammed up with the stuff."

"Thanks, dear. Buy you a drink?" A very old lady would no doubt go to bed early at night. Much preferable to a frisky young couple who might fancy a late-night swim in their skins.

"No, thanks—they're beginning to flock in as you can see. I'm off to my battle station."

Cosmo felt a hearty slap on his left shoulder; fortunately his drink was in his right hand. Arne Lund got onto the next stool and said, "I'll join you. That your first or second?"

"Second."

"A double, same thing, with Booth's, can't be left at the post," Arne said to the bartender. He was a big broadshouldered man in his sixties, gray-fair hair falling carelessly across a strong bony forehead, piercing gray eyes that looked as if they had been searching seas for decades instead of gazing at a drawing board. His manner was brusk, cynical, good-natured and without hostly mannerisms of any kind. Although his favorite cronies were fishermen and the occasional strayed-from-home New Yorker, he was, Cosmo knew, a man of fastidious, unerring taste in art, music and literature. He was also a man of power; he knew everybody of any importance in town, as well as a great many people of no importance.

After their drink he said, "Let's have a bite of fish," and they went to a corner table in the dining room. Arne's son Nils was head chef at Pepe's Wharf, internationally and superbly trained; the bite was the best swordfish steak Cosmo had ever tasted, with a salad of shaved icicle radishes, a crumble of some delectable goat cheese he couldn't identify, and a dressing so tart it caused a sting behind the ears. Arne ordered a bottle of white wine.

Cosmo thought it was time to go into his act. He toyed with his fish, putting a thumbs-down on his appetite. He sipped his wine in silence. He put the back of his hand to his forehead, started to say something, and then stopped.

"What the hell's the matter with you?" Arne asked. "You usually eat and drink for two."

"I don't know—well, yes, I do. Has any old love affair ever come back and hit you in the gut?"

Arne, emptying and refilling his own wine glass, took a few seconds for thought. "I can't say that it's happened to me the way you describe it, no. What's gone's gone. Is that why you look like a flounder gasping on the beach?"

"I've just seen her after . . . oh Christ, I don't know how many years . . ."

Is he going to burst out crying? Arne wondered with horror. The haunted dark eyes looked wet. Or was it the gin and then the wine on top of it?

Over the sound system came—one of Arne's own records, he had no use for any commercially supplied music—the waltz from Strauss's *Der Rosenkavalier.* Cosmo's hand twitched so sharply he knocked his glass over. "Not a bad idea," he said, in a voice a little above a murmur. "Not a bad idea . . ."

Arne, who had no fondness for attending on other people's emotional overflows, particularly when the lachrymose stage threatened, got rapidly to his feet. "Good luck with your idea, whatever it is. I have to get back on the job. If you're not too overcome with love and the rest of it for dessert, there's supposed to be Nesselrode pie today, everything in it so damned good and expensive we have to sell it at a loss." He winked. "Or very nearly." He gave Cosmo another clap on the shoulder and disappeared into the kitchen.

Afterward, he told his handsome Marianne, who was his partner in marriage as well as in running the restaurant, "I thought that under the role of the sensitive *artiste* he was so tough you could hammer a nail into his bicep and he'd never feel it. You never know, do you."

Cosmo, on his way back to Mrs. Oliva's, wore his gloom like a cloak, just in case someone might see him and remember. But that didn't stop him from doing several errands.

He bought an expensive but not awkwardly large box of chocolates at the Hand-Dip Bonbonnerie, and a nosegay of tight fresh apricot rosebuds in a lavish frill of lacy paper at the Windflower, also picking up an extra spool of ribbon. At the variety store next door, he bought a large paper shopping bag to hold and conceal his purchases.

Reaching his room, he temporarily removed the lacy paper so as not to get it wet and put his roses into a tumbler of water. Then, suddenly swept by a wave of exhaustion, unreality, apprehension, and drink, he undressed, pulled down the shades, went to bed and fell immediately asleep.

Waking briefly around three in the afternoon, he thought—as though continuing some mental debate that had been going on while he was asleep—well, of course, it didn't sound real but what else was there to do?

Pieces of paper with statements and/or demands on them could be torn up and thrown away; anyway, pieces of paper could be implicating, depending on how you read them. Telephones could be instantly hung up when the voice on the other end was one you refused to hear. Bolted doors could not be broken open, the violence involved calling for police response.

If the whole operation went awry in some way, even if he was spotted, stopped, in the middle of it, he was covered.

And this way, she could hardly call the police, under the circumstances.

Under his arrangement of the circumstances.

Cosmo left the Lightship a little before two. The town was not respectably and silently asleep, but then it never was; there were pockets of light, noise, laughter, music, and dissent. He went up to his room and gave himself a small helping, vigorously snorted, of the minute holdback of cocaine he kept for his own occasional use when making deliveries for Buggie.

He changed his clothes to dark pants and jersey and sneakers. Going down the stairs, he began to feel what he wanted to feel and knew he would feel: the sudden lift of what-the-hell euphoria, a sense of serene mental and physical confidence, nothing now he couldn't tackle, and tackle ably; and the freshly spurting energy of one who had just arisen from a deep long sleep.

He drove his car to within several streets of the Lilacs and parked it halfway up, in the small side lot of a closed grocery store. It was a clear dark night with no moon but stars modestly twinkling, far from their August brilliance. There was a white picket fence along the road in front of Miss Winthrop's house. He tossed himself over this and stood looking for a moment at the Lilacs. One low outside light on, over the door, for possible late guests, a dimmish light in the sitting room, probably kept on all night. The bedrooms were dark. It was now about twenty minutes of three.

In the house directly in front of him, the downstairs and upstairs were in darkness. No porch light on, it being inconceivable that May went out into the small hours merrymaking and needed illumination when arriving home; or that the old carrots-and-celery lady indulged in riotous after-hours pastimes.

He went around the side of the house, skirting the goldfish pond, to the stand of old willows at the rear. Over at the Lilacs, the sound of a child crying came through an open window. A light was snapped on. In a few minutes the crying stopped and the light went off. Cosmo stood, waiting, deep in the willows.

What a sight he'd make, he thought, pleased that he was detached enough to be amused; what a sight if the child's bedroom light had found him, which it couldn't have. A box of chocolates tied to his belt with a length of pink ribbon. A nosegay of rosebuds in frilled paper tied with ribbon around his neck and resting on his chest.

He listened to the sleeping house for another several minutes. Not a sound from inside.

The tide was going out and the water was quiet.

He had an excellent visual memory and thought he knew the tree he wanted, solid, climbable, with several long twisted heavy boughs that ran more or less horizontally, with only a slight upward angling, at the height of the second floor of the house. He began to climb.

It was a necessarily slow ascent because he wanted to maintain the closest possible thing to absolute silence, no rustle of leaves, no snapping of dead twigs. Now the last stage: he started his crawl along the upward-tilting limb that would carry him to within about three feet of the center window in the house wall.

On his first visit here, the bedroom door had been open

and the room lamplit. He recalled a glimpse showing a bed against, from the living room, the far wall, its brass head against the corner angle of the wall. That would place the window, this window, a foot or so beyond the end of the bed. Good. It would hardly do to tumble heavily across the sleeping May.

As in many houses by the sea, the windows were unscreened; had been downstairs, anyway, in the suite. In case May's window had a screen to be dealt with, he had brought a razor blade for a small cut or slash close to the latch, but he was relieved to find he wouldn't need the blade. The sash window was raised three feet from the sill. No screen.

He was now kneeling on the bough, holding on with one hand to the branch overhead. He tossed his nosegay back over his shoulder, reached out the other hand to the sill, locked his fingers underneath its inside extension, then releasing the branch let his other arm fall forward and his other hand grasp the sill. With a tremendous thrust of his torso and knees, he went through the window, almost like a winged and not a legged creature, and landed as he knew he would, flat on the floor on his face, the sounds of his entry thundering in his ears.

FIFTEEN

There was a not-quite-human sound from the head of the bed, in the corner against the wall, somewhere between a gurgle and a grunt. There was a convulsive rustle and fling of bedcoverings.

He rolled swiftly to his feet and clamped his hand over her mouth. He could feel the terror coming up from the bed at him.

"I come in peace, May," he said, his voice calm and authoritative. "What you feel is a loving and not a threatening hand. I just don't want you to scream, that's all." After a second's fumbling, he switched on the bedside lamp. "I have come for a talk, plainly and simply, nothing more—for *the* talk. We've both done enough dithering. Now we settle things."

He removed his hand, ready to fasten it to her mouth again. He untied from his belt the box of chocolates, and drew over his head the ribbon loop holding the nosegay, and put both on the bedside table.

"Let me get you a robe, you're shivering." He went to the closet, moving backward with a sure step, felt behind him after opening the door, found something long and woolly-feeling, and brought it to her. It was, his fingers accurate, a navy-blue bathrobe.

She sat rigidly up in bed and pulled it on. Then she reached over for the bedside telephone. Something about his powerful calm induced an answering, desperate calm in her. "I'm going to call the police. I must warn you if you try violence that there are two people in the suite, a young man and woman."

"Wait, May. You can't very well call the police. Here's what you would have to tell them. The husband you deserted and who has been searching for you for years—lovingly—has finally found you."

She began dialing. He took the receiver from her hand, put it in the table drawer, and with a touch of his finger broke the connection.

"Now, this husband, this man who loves you, whom you have been too shy to see, and whom you have locked out, has in a most romantic way climbed in your window with a gift of flowers and chocolates. I don't know if you or the police know anything about opera, but that descriptive name for me, Der Rosenkavalier, might occur to the newspapers—and what a lovely story it would make. Wouldn't it? In addition, you are probably aware that one of the things the police dislike most is crashing into the middle of private domestic problems."

He stopped, watching her. She made no attempt to get the receiver out of the drawer.

"Shall we have some coffee in the other room? We might as well; we have a lot to talk about. It's only fair to make myself perfectly clear. I have no intention of giving up my part in the Lilacs—helping you to run it, sharing the profits from it. This isn't a whim of mine. It will not go away. I will not go away."

She got up off the bed. Passing the bureau, she took an ivory-backed brush to her hair. Borrow his calm, use it, defeat him with it. She made fresh coffee, and after it dripped they took their cups into the living room.

"To save you embarrassment, I'll, if you like, be Mr. Lockett," he said, and took a sip of his coffee. "Cosmo Fane having been my professional name. People accept all sorts of odd marital goings-on these days—separations, reunions, remarriages. It happens all the time. I foresee no other problems."

She too sipped her coffee. "I foresee only one. That it is out of the question." She let this statement stand alone for a moment, and drank some more of her coffee.

"I'd sell the Lilacs first, before having you on the premises. Heaven knows how many offers I've turned down." Of course, she wouldn't, ever, sell the Lilacs, but say anything, anything, say it calmly, to show him his cause is hopeless.

"Be careful, May." His voice was soft. "Be very, very careful. This is your last chance."

"My last chance for what? For destroying the rest of my life on your behalf? Or . . ." Not knowing herself at all, she got up from her chair, went into the kitchen, and came out with a graceful, wickedly sharp German carving knife. "Or were you thinking of trying to kill me, with people downstairs?"

"No, that's not what I meant. This is your last chance to save my life."

Through a curious kind of shock—because he had sounded as if he meant every word of it—she said, "Saving your life is your own business, I would think."

"Not exactly, in this case. Put down that knife, you won't need it. I have my own anyway." He touched his back pocket.

She sat down again in the chair opposite him.

"You were my only hope. You could have given me a new life." The power and confidence had slipped off like a garment fallen to the floor. His voice was low. Even though she knew him of old to be a skilled dissembler, she felt something of authentic frustration, desperation, coming through to her. "I've told you what it's been like since you left me, or rather told you about the tip of the iceberg. No, says May. Go to hell, or rather go back to hell."

He paused. She said nothing.

"While I was in your tree I fastened a very neat rope noose, about thirteen feet above the ground. Upon my leaving you, which will be soon, no point in going on with this, I shall make use of it."

He took the switchblade knife from his pocket, opened it, and scored a cut across the heel of his palm. Blood rose and poured along his wrist. May had always been terrified, he knew, at the sight of even a drop of blood.

"*No . . .* no, Cosmo!"

He wrapped a handkerchief around the wound, which instantly began to soak through. "I'm not afraid of pain any more, I'm not afraid of anything any more, of death . . . you've given me good reasons not to be afraid of that. I'm sorry, but I think there will be a great deal of excitement at the Lilacs when a man is found hanging from your tree. By the way, I left a letter in my room to be opened in the morning in case I hadn't returned by then. It tells our story—our marriage, your leaving me—in toto, and explains that in case you again refuse a reunion, I will take the only course open to me. There's no point in your trying to stop me, by the way. All it is is out the window, head in the noose, drop the feet, and that's that, I believe death takes about one or two minutes and no help you could try to summon could possibly delay or prevent it."

Frantic brain, telling her, all right, give in, then later sell out, her share at least, and go away, far away.

Or give the *appearance* of surrender.

Frantic voice, over the thunderstorm of heartbeats, defeat and weariness in the voice too, "All right. You win. But I'll need a few days—there are several other shareholders, Miss Winthrop's nieces. I'll have to clear it with them, explain it in my own way . . . it's awkward, after all . . . They'd have to know and agree before the legal papers are drawn up." He would have no way of knowing that the shareholding nieces were an invention.

Vivid color that hinted at returning life and hope surged up under his skin. "How long would that take?"

"Today's Monday, give me until, say, Thursday. The nieces live here on the Cape, so it's a matter of a little driving, that's all."

"Do me two favors. Let me borrow a couple of your handkerchiefs for my hand, or some bandaging if you have it. And let me have something in writing."

"Why? Do you think I'll run away and leave behind my entire world? You can check me by phone to see I'm still here. And the something in writing won't mean anything without the nieces' consent. No, I will not do that."

Cosmo hesitated, then decided not to press the point. She looked on the edge of collapse, she might go into hysterics, change her mind, tell him in so many words to go hang himself.

She brought him disinfectant, a roll of bandaging, scissors, and tape. He could see from the way she walked her legs would hardly hold her. He did a quick workmanlike job on his hand.

"I'll go now. The tree's the best way, so that I can take the noose off. And I will be in touch, of course, now that we've made our pact." He smiled. "Signed in blood, you might say. When you're off contacting your—our—shareholders leave a message to that effect." He got up and patted her on the shoulder. "Good night, May."

She could hardly believe that her apartment was empty of him, that her life was her own again.

For a few days.

For a few days?

She dragged herself to the window he had come in and left by. She peered out into the night, but she had been too slow. Not a sound, no sense of movement in the tree. He was gone.

So she wouldn't have been able to check, if she had had the speed and the brains and a flashlight, whether there ever had been a noose, hanging waiting in the tree.

Lou Aveiro had no hesitation about calling Buggie out of his slumbers at close to four in the morning. He had an idea that Buggie conducted most of his business at night anyway. And he might get his knuckles rapped, holding onto this until morning.

Buggie answered on the second ring, no blur of the roused sleeper in his alert voice. "Lou. Anything?"

"Anything! He parks his car a couple of blocks away from the Lilacs a little after half past two, and gets out. He takes his time, stopping and listening, not moving very fast. That gave *me* time to circle around and get behind one of the cars in the parking lot on the other side of the Winthrop house and—"

"I'm not interested in your technique. You have a job to do and you do it. What happened?"

"He climbed a tree until he got near a window in the second story, where Lockett lives. He threw himself in at the window. After a minute or so the light went on. He was in the place all in all about twenty-five minutes. The living room and kitchen lights went on too—I've done electrical work there so I know the layout. Then finally the bedroom light went out and he came out of the window into the tree and climbed down. I'm not sure, but I think he had something white in his hand, or wrapped around it. He went back to his car and drove to Mrs. Oliva's and went up the side stairs to his room. The light went on there, but it only stayed on for about ten minutes. I heard the window being opened wider, and then nothing, I guess he went to bed. Should I stay on his heels or what?"

"Yes, until I tell you to lay off."

Aveiro didn't know or particularly care what the man he had been following was up to: his job was reporting and not puzzling things out. The thought crossed his mind, however, that he couldn't imagine Lockett with a lover.

Buggie didn't know exactly what Cosmo was up to either, but he cared a great deal about exactly what it might be.

The one hundred and seventy-five dollar a day suite at the Lilacs. The dead of night secret visit to Mrs. Lockett of the Lilacs.

Cosmo didn't have any business connection with the Lilacs. He did have a business connection with the Lightship. And another one with him, Buggie.

SIXTEEN

The endless sleepless night finally over, Mrs. Lockett caught sight of her ravaged face in the mirror and realized something would have to be done about it. She didn't want people talking about how tired, how strange, she looked that week in July when . . .

She took aspirin, soaked in a hot bath, applied a touch of rarely used makeup, put on a crisp pink-and-white-striped dress, drank two cups of tea made at double the usual strength, and went out into the seven o'clock freshness of the morning. The air would help too.

She often took a turn at cutting flowers for the breakfast table, a pleasant fragrant task. Nasturtiums would be nice this morning, rimmed around with a flicker of white sweet alyssum—but then she remembered the white lacy paper around the apricot rosebuds and picked cream and yellow columbine instead.

In the kitchen, she arranged her nosegays in the little glass pitchers for each table, wanting to chat with great vivacity and obvious cheer to Mrs. Captiva, who was busy at the stove. But she could find nothing to say except that it was a lovely morning and that while she was in the garden a robin had hopped along to within five feet of her. "That's nice," Mrs. Captiva said, flipping the buttermilk pancakes on the griddle. "Reminds me I want to pick up a chicken to roast for dinner. They're on sale at Cudworth's."

Mrs. Lockett was very much relieved to see Major Yard-

ley seating himself at his regular window table at eight.
What if he had been ill today? But he was never ill. What if
it had been raining, too heavily for his walk? But it was a
glorious day.

A man of blessedly regular routine, the major always
returned to his cottage after breakfast to read the Boston
Globe, which he had delivered daily, then to work for a
while in his little vegetable garden. After that, on most
days, he would be off for his march to the Town Hall.

Unless he had errands, a haircut, shopping to do, he was
usually away for half an hour to thirty-five minutes. Which
ought to provide her with plenty of time.

She came to his table to say good-morning, and he said,
"To wish myself a happy birthday—as it is, today, my
birthday, I mean—I hereby invite you to dinner tonight at
the Lightship with me."

He misinterpreted, and was pleased by, Mrs. Lockett's
suddenly rising color. By God, it was nice to see a woman
blush at a man's attentions, they so seldom did that any
more.

"Well, I . . . heavens! Thank you, how kind. I've invited a friend to dinner tonight, though . . . perhaps
later in the week?" But not the Lightship, never the
Lightship. And if she went out someplace else for dinner
with him, say Pepe's Wharf, would she have to report the
reason for her absence to the man who would, he said, be
making phone checks to see she hadn't fled?

"I'll look forward to it, just let me know the day." After
his leisurely breakfast, he left the room and she saw him
heading back to the west cottage. As it was his birthday,
would he have visitors, people bringing presents, would
he *not* take his walk this morning? But while he had acquaintances in town, she doubted close, gift-giving
friends.

No; there, at ten-thirty, he went, down the path and

through the arch. She went to the linen closet and took out a freshly laundered blue bath mat, a normal, housekeeperly thing to be carrying about.

Not that she had anything to fear, being seen anywhere in the inn or at the cottages. She was a fixture of the Lilacs landscape.

She went to the cottage, which was to the left of the terrace, one-story white clapboard with a large attic under the peaked roof, facing the water through a sheltering stand of old wind-bent cedars. From the large ring in her handbag, which held keys to every door, every drawer, every lock in the Lilacs, she selected the key to his front door.

There was no reason to listen for the clattering arrival of the cleaning cart outside. In summer, the major's cottage was always cleaned between eleven-fifteen and twelve. That was the time when, in fair weather, he liked to sun himself on the terrace, sip a long scotch-and-soda, and take a dip in the water, even at low tide ("All that walking on wet sand is good for a man's leg muscles"). When the weather was inclement, he spent his pre-lunch hour in the inn sitting room, often having the luck to find a man with whom to discuss the war; any war would do.

Several summers ago, when she had dropped by one morning to see whether the major's slipcovers needed laundering, he had invited her to sit down and have a cup of coffee with him. "I keep instant here, not as good as yours, but it's handy. Something happened last night I wanted to tell you about."

A little after midnight, the major had looked out his bedroom window to see the moon on the water and fastened his gaze instead on a shiny eerie black figure climbing the steps out of the sea. He got his 45-gauge service pistol, put it in his bathrobe pocket, and went out to challenge the intruder, who was in a skindiving suit. He had said sternly, "This is private property, these stairs are not for public use, and least of all at this hour of the night. Unless—are you a guest here?"

No, the young man had said, adding that he didn't mean any harm and had just wanted to get over to Commercial Street and thought this would be a handy shortcut. "Well, use somebody else's shortcut," ordered Major Yardley, and the black-suited figure obediently descended the steps and plunged into the water. The major watched at his window for half an hour but there was no reappearance to deal with.

He had, after bringing Mrs. Lockett her cup of coffee, gone into his bedroom and brought out the pistol. "When I think of all the unprotected women and children here I'm glad I've got this old friend by me," he said. "Not that there aren't the men too, of course, but I doubt they're armed, in fact I'd very much hope not."

She gazed at the object in horror; firearms terrified her. He saw the look on her face and said, "It's perfectly safe. Here, I'll show you how it works." She realized he was proud of his gun, proud of the confident dexterity of his fingers, handling it. "You just cock it, then push this slide back, and then you pull the trigger. A new bullet moves automatically into place when you fire your first bullet. They can say what they like about weapons, but give me the good old 45-gauge service pistol every time."

Was he reliving glory, the most dramatic time of his life? His face glowed with affection for his gun. She thought that in some male, military way he was pleased and flattered by her fear of it. "Here, you're just the same as most women, you're afraid it'll take it into its head to go off by itself. I'll put it back, but I thought you'd like to know there's real protection at hand, at the Lilacs, every month of the year."

It would be a reasonable guess that he still kept it somewhere in his bedroom. Feeling horribly nervous and guilty, she went in to search.

If he came back unexpectedly, she would be doing her slipcover check again. As a matter of fact, the chintz cover on the armchair by the window looked as if it could do with laundering. Should she take it off and be carrying it over her arm, in case he or anyone else came in? Susan and Maria had keys to the cottage too.

No, don't waste another minute, concentrate on the job. Concentrate on the theft.

She went swiftly through the big chest of drawers, careful not to untidy the folded shirts, shorts, balled-up clean socks, undershorts. Would it be in a box of some kind, or wrapped in a handkerchief? Her fingers encountered no box, or anything that felt like an automatic pistol.

The bedside table? The logical place, probably, at least in books she had read, but it seemed too easy, too quick a solution. She found on her ring the bedside table key. There were two drawers. Somehow the secret unlocking of the drawers, the tiny furtive sounds, made her feel even guiltier.

The top drawer held a silver flask, a small packet of paper tissues, and a little leather jeweler's box that probably held cuff links—or would it be ammunition? She opened the box and found gold cuff links on a bed of cotton.

Oh God—fingerprints. Or did it matter? There must be thousands of her prints everywhere in the Lilacs. If the girls cleaned properly, and didn't skimp, all the wood surfaces in the room would be sprayed and buffed shiny again.

The second drawer held a Bible, a tarnished Army identification bracelet, and an oblong well-polished mahogany box. The box wasn't locked. She lifted the lid and saw the pistol. She picked it up with shrinking fingers and put it in her handbag, and closed and relocked the drawer.

She retrieved from the bed the rolled bath mat and left the cottage, feeling even more strongly the need for secrecy and speed, by the back door in the small kitchen. She made herself linger for a few minutes, in case eyes, anyone's eyes, might be watching, and forced herself to an interested examination of the major's six tomato plants, row of lettuce, and third row of carrots and what looked like radishes. Then she rounded the side of the cottage and went along the short curved path in the cedars that led to the terrace.

As this was to look, outwardly, like a cottage-checking morning, she went to the east cottage near the other end of the terrace. A blue bath mat might well be needed here, an innocent errand done. The cottage was temporarily empty, its occupants having left Monday morning. A man and his wife and two children, the name Reeves, would arrive here in midafternoon.

She heard a sound from the bathroom and almost cried out. Susan appeared in the bathroom doorway. "We were short of towels when I did the cleanout yesterday morning and I—" She stopped. Her blue eyes looked very wide and for a second or so seemed to come closer, retreat, enlarge, under Mrs. Lockett's gaze.

"Are you all right?" Susan asked in soft concern. She reached out a supporting hand and took Mrs. Lockett's arm. Later she told Dominic, "For a moment I was terrified, I thought she was going to faint, or have a heart attack, she didn't look herself at all."

"No . . . perhaps a touch of indigestion, or coming in from the bright sun, it's so shadowy here in the morning . . . I wanted to check the bath mat . . ."

Fumbling to unroll it, she dropped her handbag. It fell on the strip of hardwood floor between the living room rug and the bathroom doorway. It fell with what sounded to her like a deafening crash. The weight of the gun, of course. She and Susan knocked their heads together as they both bent for the handbag. Mrs. Lockett seized a strap before Susan's hand could touch the soft leather bag, maybe even get a feel of what was inside it.

How awful all this was. What awful things Cosmo was making her do. This wasn't she, this near-fainting woman babbling of indigestion and sun and shadow.

"Sit down and let me get you a drink of water," Susan said, still anxious.

"No, I'm fine." She went into the bathroom and inspected the mat beside the tub. Must repair herself, repair this little betraying damage done in front of Susan. "Well, it looks al*most* . . . but my grandmother used to say, There's no such thing as almost clean, if it isn't clean it's dirty." She replaced the dark blue mat with the light blue.

Could Susan have seen her from the windows here, coming along the path from Major Yardley's cottage? And what if she had? Don't pursue, in this way, every frailest spidery thread, or she would drive herself mad.

"Remember to see there's a nice bowl of roses on the coffee table when the Reeves family gets here, Susan," she said, and turned and went in a deliberately unhurried manner past the inn, across the street, and up the stairs to her own rooms, her own lair.

"Yes," Mrs. Captiva said to the man on the telephone, "yes, she's here, but not in the office at the moment, is there any message?" She thought the voice was vaguely familiar but was much too busy this morning to attempt to pin it down.

"No, just tell her," with a little chuckle, "a cavalier called."

Mrs. Lockett's first thought when she considered her hiding place for the pistol was to put it at the bottom of one of Ann Winthrop's boxes of neatly folded clothes, in the attic.

But there, it would be too inaccessible if she needed it in a hurry. And, she added mentally in a self-hypnotizing way, she might never need it at all. After distraught wandering from kitchen to bedroom to sitting room, she settled on the rack of a seldom used countertop broiler-oven, which she kept in the ample cabinets under the kitchen counter.

Police would probably look in female hiding places like shoeboxes, or under the mattress, or in one of the drawers of the dressing table beneath half a dozen pairs of neatly arranged gloves, or in a bureau drawer among slips and bras and girdles and stockings.

Police? What police? Why?

Who would ever suspect that Mrs. Lockett of the Lilacs had stolen anything from a guest, much less a gun? Had committed—for the first time in her life—an actual, prosecutable crime?

Crime? Mrs. Lockett? Never.

Perhaps another cup of tea; she still felt odd, not at all herself. (Her mind, it occurred horribly to her, like a scuttling terrified small animal, a rodent, seeking a savage surviving bite here, or dark shelter and safety there in perhaps another corner.) She made the tea, and sitting in her chair, from which she had a view of the west cottage, saw while she was drinking it the major striding along the path to his violated quarters.

A brief panic seized her. What if he cleaned and oiled his gun, say, once every month, or two months, on a given day? What if this was the day? She could envision his hand unlocking the drawer, lifting the lid of the box, and finding it empty. He would, of course, raise the roof. He would, of course, notify the police. He would, of course, suspect first of all the staff, Dominic, Maria, Mrs. Captiva, Susan.

Susan, hauled on the carpet, saying hesitantly, even reluctantly, that she hadn't seen anyone but Mrs. Lockett, coming away from the west cottage at about ten minutes of eleven . . .

Drop this fantasy, drop it immediately. Go back, far back, to the mind-stopped calm she had felt after the blow Cosmo struck her, after she had taken matters into her own hands and ended the danger, ended the marriage.

Just, at that time, going about doing what had to be done, quietly, neatly. The packing, the move to the hotel room, the train to Boston, the orderly selection of Provincetown and the Lilacs as a place to settle in, the steady remaking of her own life, and doing it—panic and pain pushed aside, not allowed to interfere—with the utmost efficiency and success.

SEVENTEEN

"Is Dominic still playing Romeo under your empty balcony?" Maria billowed a white sheet across the bed and Susan caught the edges on her side and began tucking them in.

"We're good friends," Susan said. "We do enjoy each other's company so much. He's very interesting when he talks about the writers he likes."

"Well, just friends, that's okay then." Maria had a strong sense of family loyalty and was extremely fond of her brother, but none of this showed in her casual bed-making chat. "You're probably wise to sit around and grow older. Dom's not like that, though, he's always in a hurry to get around the next corner. Well, so am I, I suppose, family trait."

Susan, head bent, listened closely while she slipped a pillow into its white case.

"As a matter of fact, he's sort of medium-hot the last few days on the trail of a girl who's just started singing at the Merry Whaler. Name's Sandra, I think. Dark red hair, blue eyes something like yours . . . I think this bedspread needs changing. See that spatter of spots down near the end?"

Susan was very thoughtful while she vacuumed the rug and then spray-polished the wood surfaces. It was Maria's turn to do the bathroom. All very well, she mused, to have Dominic as a friend, but to *lose* Dominic as a friend—well, that was a different kind of thing entirely. It would be like being very thirsty, even thirstier than you'd realized, and having someone rudely snatch away the glass of restoring, essential water just as you were raising it to your lips.

After she had finished her day's work, at four, she bicycled into town, bought a birthday present for her mother, did several more errands, and then went home to Parasol Street. She showered and dressed, taking from the closet the prettiest thing she owned, a loose-topped oyster silk shantung dress with smocking around the neck and a graceful rippling skirt, not a Provincetown kind of dress at all. Her heeled black sandals ought to go nicely with it. A little perfume, Patou's *Joy*, which Daniel had given her for Christmas several years ago and which, when the breakup came, she thought about throwing away, but it was too expensive for that.

The phone beside her bed rang. She looked at her watch. Only six o'clock. Much too early. It was Bart Young, whom she had met through Maria, wanting to take her to dinner to a new place he'd heard about in Dennisport. She conveyed a thank-you and the fact that she was busy tonight. Her apology was so soft and mannerly that he took it as the next best thing to acceptance.

Time stretched out after that. She read a library book Dominic had recommended to her attention, Maria Dermoût's *The Ten Thousand Things*, and too fluttery inside for any real appetite, nibbled a few cheese crackers from her emergency collection of edibles on the closet shelf.

She rebrushed her hair and touched her eyelids with a faint gloss of lavender-blue. After eight o'clock now, but it felt as if it ought to be ten. The phone rang again.

Dominic said, "Oh good, you're there. I have a message to deliver to you, a telegram which was phoned in here instead of to your place while I was on office duty. Will you be in for a while?"

"Yes. A *telegram?* Not . . . bad news from home?"

"No, nothing about your family. It's sort of private, though, the message. I don't suppose you're receiving in your bedroom?"

"Certainly not. There's a nice quiet back porch here, usually unoccupied."

"I'll meet you there in ten minutes."

Susan brushed her hair a third time and went downstairs to the porch, which was bordered by tall white-scented night stock. Wistaria vines swayed like long curtains from the porch roof. If shabby, it was a romantic place now in the evening light. The glider, which would hold two comfortably, would look too obvious. She sat down in a webbed white plastic chair.

It was only nine minutes, not ten, by her watch, when Dominic came around the corner of the house and up the steps. His eyes in the brown face always looked vivid but now even more so, burningly dark. He sat on the porch rail, near her, and took a slip of paper from his pocket.

"You'll never be able to read this, Susan, I have a few scraps of shorthand left but I mostly abbreviate. You look very nice, were you expecting someone?"

"Not really. I don't like to rush you but, if you could get to the telegram . . ."

He got to it immediately.

"Susan dear, first I have to apologize for what happened in February, I know now I was crazy. It didn't take me long to find out how wrong I was and that you are the most important thing in the world to me. I'm back on my own now, have been for two months, trying to get up my courage to get in touch with you and say please forget and forgive." Dominic's voice was low and vibrant, and without any kind of dramatic emphasis. "Please, please send a note or letter, or telegram, as the phone here is often busy, and I will be up there in Provincetown like a shot. In fact, I will be up like a shot in a week if I don't hear from you and will put my case in person. Love and hugs, and, no matter what you say right off, kisses too, from your own Daniel."

After a short silence, Susan said a little breathlessly, "You took that down very well, Dominic, for such a long message."

He got off the rail and went to sit on the glider across from her, a few feet away. In a pondering fashion, he said, "In the kind of words you use, I don't know as I'd put much or any reliance on an inconstant man like that."

Susan sat up very straight in her chair. "What do *you* mean, inconstant?"

"What do you mean by what do I mean?"

"How about you? Maria just dropped it accidentally . . . a girl at the Merry Whaler that you . . ." A rush of pink had come up under the light honeyed tan of her skin. She felt a little giddy with the heavy scent of the stock.

Dominic's eyes, holding hers, burned an even fiercer brown. *"Friends* can't be accused of being inconstant. Only lovers can. Or people tied close together. Maybe we'd better stop being friends."

"Stop being . . . ?" Was it all going to backfire on her? Serve her right, she thought, in a flash of foreseeing wretchedness.

"And go on to—" He stood up, reached for her hand, and pulled her urgently to her feet and to him. Arms hard and close around her, he kissed her tentatively and then with entire conviction. It took him quite a while to finish his sentence. ". . . to wherever we've been heading all along. To right here."

The screen door from the house opened. Seeing the locked pair, a woman said, "Oh, I *am* sorry . . ." and retreated, but neither of them heard her. His lips moving against the skin of her neck, making a delightful sort of tingle, he said, "By the way, do you think I would have delivered that telegram in person if I didn't think—if I wasn't almost sure—I could beat him at his own game?"

Susan lifted her head, gave him a charming smile, and moved a caressing hand against his back. "Do you think that if I didn't think you could I would have sent myself that telegram?"

In her arms, Dominic began to shake with laughter. "I see," he murmured, "that we have two writers in the family."

EIGHTEEN

Buggie, on this Tuesday afternoon, found himself curiously unable to concentrate in the silence of his own apartment on Audley's Wharf. The sun was directly overhead, and the water sent quivers of swimming light all over the ceiling. Distracting. What he needed was noise and bustle to get his head going.

He went down to Sub Rosa's, comfortably dark after upstairs, inside shutters partially closed. It was as usual crowded, not a man in the place except himself, women dancing together, drinking, chattering or sitting in silence, hard rock crashing through the sound system. No style, no class to Rosa's dikes, in Buggie's detached opinion; bunch of truckdrivers and stevedores with breasts. But the dark and vaguely sinister scene was the atmosphere he wanted for thinking things out. Thinking Cosmo out.

Rosa came over to his table. She was middle-aged, with a circular face that looked like a plate that had fallen on the floor and been put inaccurately and crookedly back together with unreliable glue.

"Bring the usual, did you?" she asked.

"I left it in your office on the way in."

"I'll be up later when the cash register needs a good emptying. Scotch today, or Pernod?"

"Pernod."

Start, Buggie said to himself, with the simplest theory. Was Cosmo planning to hand him over to someone, no doubt for money? That two A.M. visit to a pillar of the community, Mrs. Lockett, through a window. Why through the window? What was the something white in or on his hand? To him, this behavior of Cosmo's was unexplainable, and anything going on in his business that couldn't be explained sent out waves of red light like the roof flasher on a police car.

Now enlarge the theory. Say that Cosmo was an investigating agent. Hadn't by chance become acquainted with him, Buggie, in New York in the late spring, in the Eighth Avenue bar where Buggie spent a good deal of his time when visiting New York; but, instead, had sought him out, there. Say that the Lightship job, the piano and all that, was a cover, and a hell of a good solid one.

Move the theory over sideways. Cosmo could be in the hire of another, and considerably larger than Buggie's, outfit in, say, Boston or New Bedford, the outfit interested in taking over the lucrative Cape and Nantucket trade, which was almost exclusively Buggie's. Of course they knew about him, but they'd have no idea how his system worked, who worked for him, what his contacts were, who and where his clients were, and the logistics of his delivery system. Cosmo, of course, being by now in an ideal position to supply an accurate blueprint.

Last but not least, it wasn't inconceivable that Cosmo was planning to set up for himself and take over the business when he had mastered all the details. Only one obstacle to be removed from his path: Buggie. If he were in Cosmo's place, he could think of only one way to cope with that inconvenience. Death. The body never found; again, if he were Cosmo, that would be the only way to play it. What ever happened to good old Buggie?

If it hadn't been for a trick movement of the tide, Ron McCallister's body might never have been found. And even found, the body hadn't pointed its finger at Buggie, the case was all but forgotten, dropped, even if it was still open on the police files. Ron had just been edging into his own subcontracting, his own little private firm, when Buggie caught him at it.

If Ron had the guts to try, local little-guy Ron, why not Cosmo, by far Ron's superior in brain and nerve and skilful handling of the slippery operation, whenever and whatever it was?

Would it be a good idea to try, right away, a little forcing of Cosmo's hand? Alveiro could follow Cosmo everywhere he went and report on everything Cosmo did, but he couldn't walk into Cosmo's head and take a good look around in there.

Trip Cosmo into some stumbling, startled explanation, or faked-up denial, or find instead an obvious show of innocence, innocence in this matter at least. You hardly, Buggie thought with sour amusement, find people of the highest moral character willing to undertake this line of work for him.

Move, Buggie, act. Instead of just sitting around waiting until another forcing hand descends with a chop on the back of your own neck? Bait your rod, dangle it, see if there was a bite or the fish spitting out the hook. *Or* see if there wasn't a fish of any kind swimming around in this particular pool.

He drank a second Pernod, pocketed a bespattered slip of paper on the table, which was the drinks list, and paid his bill. He went back to his apartment, pulled on a pair of thin rubber gloves, and on the blank back of the drinks list printed, with his left hand, "How would you like to join Ron McCallister in a nice big Drink?"

He telephoned Mrs. Oliva's, asked for Cosmo, and was told he was out. Good. He strolled over to the Bayview Lodge, went up the outside stairs, and slid the piece of paper under Cosmo's closed door. Admittedly—properly interpreted—the note was a loaded one, but if in the remote case its delivery came under police check and he had been observed climbing the stairs, he would say he was just leaving it there on request from some woman, he didn't know her name, at Sub Rosa's. However, he could hardly see Cosmo going to the police with Exhibit A and telling them that he saw this unsigned note as a threat from Buggie. And what, the police would ask, did Buggie have to threaten Cosmo about?

Halfway down the stairs, he met Margaret Rudd, coming up, carrying a cello case.

Waking yesterday morning, after a bad night, she began to feel a sick regret and remorse. Having vented her rage, there was none of it left to strengthen and sustain her.

Had he found anywhere to sleep, in this filled-up holiday town? Or stretched out on a bench in the chill damp of the night waiting for the first ferry in the morning?

The way she had arranged things, she told herself bitterly, meant that she would probably never see him again, the most important person in her life.

And that lovely expensive lunch he had bought her at Totter's . . . and Jean Latimer's story about seeing him with Claudine on the porch was probably embroidered, blown-up, out of jealousy. After all, making not much money, why shouldn't he have lunch with a friend instead of paying for it at a restaurant?

Walking distractedly back and forth in her house, rumpling her hair with a hand that was half frantic and half punishing, she saw, lying on the floor under the table beside the sofa, his cello case. He had been so stunned with anger at her that he had walked off without it. She lifted it to the sofa and opened it. Here, in a ghostly way, was Cosmo, or the sound of Cosmo. She stroked the satiny wood with tender fingers. Lovely lining to the case, if a bit shabby, royal purple velvet. His initials in worn gold at the handle.

By midafternoon, she had made up her mind. This was a valuable instrument and ought to be in the possession of its owner. What if her house was burgled or something before he came back next weekend to collect it? Or, more probably, sent someone else, a stranger, to collect it.

The practical, sensible thing to do, from every point of view, was to bring it to him in Provincetown. Show him her contribution. Show him what trouble she was willing to take on his behalf, no effort too great for her own Cosmo.

He might even need it during the week for some reason, some performance, and be too embarrassed (dismiss the thought of his being still too angry) to call her. She discarded the idea of calling him and saving herself the trip; too cold, too much suggesting that she'd like him to get every last vestige of himself out of her house.

Later would be better, tomorrow, than earlier. She had no idea when he got up in the morning after the long stint at the Lightship, and what he did with himself during the day. But middle to late afternoon ought to be a good choice, he would probably return home to shower and change for the evening as he did weekends here.

Besides, the free morning would give her time to have her hair done, and look her freshest and her best, for Cosmo.

Buggie recognized the cello case from a faint chalklike smear at one end, but such identification seemed hardly necessary here on Cosmo's stairway. He also noted sharply the extreme nervousness, perhaps even fear, emanating from this woman.

"If you're looking for Cosmo, he's out," he said. "I see that's his cello you're returning to him."

"Oh dear. Out." She looked even more uncertain. "I don't know quite what to . . ."

In as amiable and natural a manner as he could summon, Buggie said, "I'm a friend of his. George Eden. If you'd like to leave it with me, I'll hand it over to him, I expect to see him tomorrow."

"Oh no, thank you, it's too valuable, I couldn't possibly entrust—" Her unwillingness to leave the instrument with a friend of Cosmo's could be read as damning, if your mind was following a certain path.

Determined on answering his own questions about her, Buggie pressed on. "Are you a P-towner? I don't think we've met before." A prod here might come in handy. "I thought I knew all his, uh, attractive circle."

She blushed. "No, I live in Nantucket, where Cosmo plays on weekends, you know. He came to my house on Sunday afternoon to give a performance for a few friends and left this precious thing behind . . ."

As he had introduced himself it was only polite to do the same; to, in some way, restore to herself a semblance of composure. "I'm Mrs. Rudd, Mrs. John Rudd."

Was her visit the beginning, or continuation of, some new two-way traffic, Nantucket to the Cape, under Cosmo's control?

"Well, the only thing I can suggest is that you wait until he shows up at seven at the Lightship," Buggie said. "Unless you'd like to check some of his other contacts. He chose the word, contacts, deliberately. She might well pass it along to Cosmo and it could give him a bad shaking up. "Like, the hostess at the Lightship, Claudine Merriman, or Mrs. Lockett out at the Lilacs, that would make a start, they're both in the phone book. Good luck." He passed her and went down the stairs.

Contacts. What a strange word to use. A word suggesting the doing of business. Did they, too, these women, pay for Cosmo's loving companionship?

Her remaining few shreds of courage fell away. Pursue him, through these women, all over town, burdened with his heavy awkward case?

Or wait for him at the Lightship? But she remembered how something about his manner frightened her when she had surprised him there before.

Without consciously arriving at her decision, she turned and went carefully down the stairs, legs feeling funny. She opened the screen door of the porch and knocked at the closed front door. The dumpy little dark-eyed woman inside said, "Sorry, we're full up, if you were looking for a place to stay."

"No. I'm returning Cosmo Fane's cello, he left it behind." No need to say more, she had done enough explaining to strangers. "Will you see that he gets it?"

"I certainly will. He wouldn't want to be without it. As he's not here right now to thank you, I'll say it for him. Shall I tell him who it was brought it back?"

"No, he'll know."

As Cosmo was by now constitutionally unable to stay in one place for more than ten minutes to half an hour, it was six o'clock before he retrieved his cello.

Several times during the day he had driven past the Lilacs. The first time, her car was missing from the parking lot. The second time, three hours later, it was there.

Only two more days of this to get through, this painful treading on hot bricks. By Thursday, she had said. Or, give me until Thursday. Did that mean Thursday morning? Or evening? Or, the torturing recurring thought, ever?

Had she been seeing, while her car was missing, one or both of the niece-shareholders? The nieces were another thing to be nervous about. What portion of the income of the Lilacs did they get? How many shares did they own, what were they worth?

By five o'clock, he couldn't stand these questions any longer. He went to a public phone booth a short distance from the Lilacs and, wondering as he dialed whether this might be some sort of fatal rocking of his boat, stopped in mid-dialing and then the finger, obsessive, began again.

She herself answered the phone. "Mrs. Lockett, the Lilacs."

"May? Quick little inquiry, I won't keep you." Get the sound of apology out of his voice. "I've been wondering, naturally enough, about those two shareholders of yours. Do their holdings amount to a great deal, or what?"

The cold sweat began to dry and he relaxed in surprise and relief at her calm matter-of-factness. "Actually, it was just a courtesy on Miss Winthrop's part. They each receive, annually, five per cent of the net profits. They're both well off, but it was a matter of family feeling. And for the same reason Miss Winthrop stipulated in her will that in case there was to be any change or alteration in management, their consent must be secured. I saw Mrs. Garth this morning and plan to see her sister tomorrow. Of course Mrs. Garth was a bit interested in my . . . in our . . . private lives, but as she's been married three times— in any case, she gave me her agreement in writing."

With a sense of pre-celebration, of being let off the rack for at least a little while, he had a gin-and-tonic at Pirate's Walk, lingered over it in a half dream, gazing out at the water, and then headed home.

Mrs. Oliva called to him from the porch, "Some woman came by, didn't give her name, to return your cello, she said you'd know who it was. I've got it locked up safe and sound in the hall closet."

Carrying the cello up the stairs, Cosmo wondered if the returning of it by Margaret, all the way from Nantucket, was a sort of final heaving out, or a form of apology and invitation. It didn't matter which. Margaret didn't matter any more.

At least, she probably didn't.

When he unlocked and opened his door, he saw the slip of paper lying on the floor just inside. He picked it up, looked in a puzzled way at Sub Rosa's soiled drinks list, all her prices exorbitant, and then turned it over.

"How would you like to join Ron McCallister in a nice big Drink?" Buggie, of course, who else? What was bugging Buggie? Was it still the business of Cosmo throwing his money around in a recklessly showy way by staying in the Winthrop suite? That six-hour stay of a few days ago, which now seemed weeks ago?

He folded the note and put it in his wallet, smiling. He thought, What will drive Buggie a little crazy is showing no response whatever to this hazy warning or deadly threat, depending on how you looked at it.

He showered and changed and strolled to the Lightship. A little after ten, he saw out of the corner of his eye Buggie at the bar, his back to it, leaning, drink in his hand, intently watching him. Wanting to see what thirteen printed words had done to his face, to his hands?

At break time, he went over to join Buggie, carrying the drink of scotch sent by a diner to reward him for his playing of the Gershwins' "Someone to Watch Over Me."

"You're in good form tonight, Cosmo."

"Thanks. I seemed to get the impression that you were all eyes and ears, taking in every note. Somehow I never thought of you as being devoted to music."

"Speaking of notes," Buggie said very casually, "someone at Rosa's asked me to drop off a note from her, to you. In your room."

"Oh? Another music lover, maybe, although in that crew . . . No, I haven't been back to my room yet."

Alveiro had reported, "He went up the stairs carrying his cello at a little before six. Came down at ten of seven with his clothes changed."

Cosmo didn't feel comfortable with the sudden sense of an electric charge coming silently at him from Buggie.

Thank Christ that in a day or so he would no longer be in Buggie's employ.

NINETEEN

"I swear it was there, handy, right beside my bed," said Major Yardley, in a wicker chair near the office door in the sitting room. The Wednesday morning was dark and windy and rain felt imminent. There was a little tinkling of ice as he lifted his eleven-fifteen scotch and soda.

In her office, Mrs. Lockett stopped in the middle of itemizing the bill for Room 2C. For a second her heart seemed to stop too.

In what must have been the chair beside him, Mrs. Carter said teasingly, "Are you sure? I've known you to be absent-minded, Major, once in a blue moon anyway."

"Of course I'm sure. I'm always careful about belongings, my own and other people's."

The first thin rain began to patter on the office window facing east.

"And you double-checked all through the cottage?"

"Yes. Not a sign of it." Another tinkle of ice as the glass was lifted.

"Maybe when you were returning your own books yesterday you just scooped it up without thinking. After all, you'd finished it. I knew you'd like it. I myself don't care much for war stories, but it gripped me . . ."

"You may be right. I'll check the library by phone. Wouldn't want you to get a black mark for an overdue book."

Mrs. Lockett felt as if, all during this exchange, she had not breathed at all. Only, mercy of God, a book, this morning, but it could have been disaster itself sitting outside her office door.

It seemed the worst kind of folly to wait any longer, wait until Thursday, when any moment he could go looking for something else, something much more important to him than a borrowed library book.

Her heart, her nerves, her body couldn't take another blow like this, even if the blow had missed and left her outwardly intact.

She finished Room 2C's bill. Mr. and Mrs. Stein came into the office at eleven-thirty to check out. Keys returned, no money changing hands because it all went on Mr. Stein's American Express card. Thank-you's and goodbyes. One tear on Margery Stein's rose-brown cheek. "Reservations for the same time next year, Mrs. L., only make it three weeks instead of two, we love it so here."

"Yes indeed, I'll look forward to seeing you again." She was reaching for a large black-leather bound book on the shelf behind her as the Steins departed.

If there is any next year at the Lilacs, she thought.

Then, mentally, she said, I saved my life, any life that would matter to me, once before. I will save my life again.

The sense of darkness around her lifted and an odd, strong composure emerged from it. She made the Steins' reservation entry in next year's book, got up from her chair when Mrs. Captiva came in to take over the office as usual at eleven forty-five, and went over to her apartment.

She called Mrs. Oliva's and asked to speak to Cosmo Fane. If by any remote chance, later, anyone connected the call with what had happened, or what might have happened, she could fall back on a version of her previously used excuse, "A friend wanted to see if she could engage him to play at her annual garden party."

The man at the other end—probably a guest passing the

phone when it rang, shoddy poor-Boston accent—said, "I saw him go out half an hour or so ago. I'll leave your number on the pad here if you want him to call back."

Mrs. Lockett gave him the unlisted number of her apartment telephone. She almost added, "You might write 'urgent,' " and then stopped herself. Too dangerous. Surely the police could get unlisted numbers identified for them. If the occasion, any pressing occasion, should arise.

What if he didn't come back the whole livelong day?

Cosmo called at one-thirty. "Hello, May. Returning your call. It's not the number listed for the Lilacs, so I wondered . . ."

"It's my private number." Be brisk and businesslike. Be reasonably friendly, but not suspiciously and suddenly friendly. "Miss Peck, Miss Winthrop's other niece, dropped by this morning on a coincidental visit, and her consent is cleared."

Cosmo, who had been expecting on the brink of victory the possibility, ever present in his mind, of the crash of failure, gave a long sigh over the phone, which she read correctly.

"Well, I felt it was a foregone conclusion but I thought you'd be interested to know. However, the main reason I'm calling is about something a good deal more important. As we're to be working partners, we might as well begin at once, especially in the matter of rather major decisions."

"Yes, of course," Cosmo said, as close to humble as she had ever heard him. "Anything I can—"

"There's a property I'm considering as an extension of the Lilacs. Every year we have to turn away, say, one-fourth of the people who would like to stay with us." She described it to him with care and succinctness.

It was a very large house, owned by a friend of Miss Winthrop's and hers, Mrs. Chantrey, a widow, now in Europe for several months. Mrs. Chantrey had for some time been thinking about selling the house as it was too large for a woman alone. She had lost her only son a few years after her husband died. She had offered Mrs. Lockett first refusal.

"Her land abuts on mine. You can't see the house from the street, it's up the hill through scrub pine and oak and so on, well behind this house and the parking lot. There's only at the moment a sandy lane, which comes to a dead end at the house. It would be quite convenient for guests. Just a short walk here although the winding lane and the lower hills from the crest make it seem a bit longer, but I'm sure to some people the privacy would be more than worth it."

Trying to sound, through his daze of pleasure and reassurance, the hardheaded man of business, Cosmo asked, "Would the cost of the place be much of a problem?"

"We haven't talked money yet, Mrs. Chantrey and I, but as we're old friends . . . The down payment would be considerable, but then with the mortgage I'm sure it could be managed without draining our resources dry, and ought to pay us back in not all that many years. There's really only half an acre of Chantrey land, although it looks like more because of the hilltop site. Don't be put off when you see it, it began as a Colonial house and has been added to in rather eccentric ways, Federal here, Victorian there, and a touch of Southern Plantation in the front. But what might seem disadvantages are advantages too, at least five porches on different levels, a large glass-domed conservatory . . ."

She paused to let all the weight and size and scope of this sink in. She took a sip of tea. She hadn't been able to eat any lunch, waiting to hear from him, and this was her fourth cup.

The hardheaded man of business does not immediately leap with glee at the prospect of pouring money into a personally unexplored investment, Cosmo had to remind himself. "It sounds at the least an idea worth looking into."

"Yes, and I mean quite literally, and right away. Mrs. Chantrey is expected back at the end of this month. We'd want time to think things out, price things out, how many rooms—and perhaps a suite or so—we could fit into the house without basic rebuilding. I've been putting off a really practical room-by-room inspection because I've been so busy. This evening, thank heavens, I'm free. Will you meet me there at, let's see, eight o'clock, and we'll go over it inch by inch, and discuss possibilities such as—well, for instance, your idea of a restaurant, which up till now I've been resisting because it's a bit beyond my sphere of experience . . ."

At this all-or-nothing moment, she paused again. Did his silence, of only a few seconds but seeming much longer, mean some hesitation about joining her? Or was he merely thunderstruck, unable to believe that this was actually happening to him, for him?

"Of course, it would cut into your work time, at the Lightship . . . ? But under the circumstances—"

"No problem," Cosmo said vigorously.

The Lightship had ceased to exist, as of now.

"The lane is just beyond the end of the parking lot, the sign is all but buried in honeysuckle, but it's there, Knob Lane. Eight o'clock, then."

"How will we get in? Is there a caretaker or something? Or will you have a real estate person with you?"

"Mrs. Chantrey always leaves her keys in my keeping when she goes away. She's a bit too penny-pinching for any Pinkerton kind of protective service, and she knows I'll keep an eye on the house for her."

Mrs. Chantrey was real, and really in Europe. The keys in Mrs. Lockett's possession were real. The Chantrey house was real, but it was not for sale.

Mrs. Lockett had a small task to perform there in mid-afternoon.

If a body was found at Mrs. Chantrey's, of course the method of entry into a locked house would come under immediate examination.

At three o'clock, she put on her raincoat and her dark blue head scarf. It was still raining, not heavily but persistently, the clouds low and slate-colored. She took a light three-quart aluminum bucket from her kitchen cabinet. The small wild black raspberries were ripe and should (explanation at hand in case she met anybody, which seemed unlikely in this weather, on this private route) be picked before the birds got them all.

The path, which she and Miss Winthrop had always called the Berry Path, narrow and barely discernible in the undergrowth, led not straight up the hill but around one side of it. She was still and would be for the next few minutes or so on her own property. On the way along the path, she pulled off, with a garden-gloved hand, the small sweet fruits which in her Connecticut childhood were called blackcaps.

Nearing the top of the hill, she reached the heavy grove ring of great weeping Norway pines which surrounded the house and made it all but invisible. Once through the pines, you were on a grass lawn, almost ready now for mowing. Every other Saturday, an old man named Aaron Vell mowed and tidied the property and made a cursory check of doors and windows.

The house loomed immense and gloomy in the rain, in

the darkness of the pines. No rhyme or reason to the house, with its mixed brew of architectural styles, but somehow impressive anyway, making a statement of comfort and amplitude and a lost, protecting security.

The front entrance showed what she had described to Cosmo as a touch of Southern Plantation, a wide long porch two stories high, roofed, with four mighty carved-wood Corinthian columns. She went around the side of the house to the original front door of the Colonial core, a modest graceful entrance, the door painted white with window-lights on either side and a fanlight above.

Several weeks ago, Aaron Vell had reported dutifully to her, "One of the panes in the light at the right side of the door is loose, putty all dried out, wants reglazing. I don't do glass work, you might want to have it seen to or again you might not. Hardly anybody uses that door anyway." She had forgotten about this small matter until she was drinking her third cup of tea, waiting for Cosmo's telephone call.

The loose pane was about a foot and a half above the doorknob. No reach at all for a man's arm, hand seeking the inside knob, which when turned would unlock the door.

She saw that her right-hand garden glove was a bit purple-stained at the fingertips. She switched gloves, putting the left-hand one on backward, and shoved strongly at the pane, which was about ten inches square. It fell inward with no sound of breaking. As she remembered, there was an oval rag rug inside, in front of the door.

The wind high in the pines was a little disturbing. If there was anyone nearby, you wouldn't be able to hear a sound, a human kind of sound.

She turned, went quickly back through the trees at the

Berry Path, and switched her gloves again to their proper hands. When she got back to the Lilacs, wet through, chilled, shivering inside but not yet on the outside, her pail held a respectable half-quart of blackcaps.

TWENTY

Cosmo called Claudine in the afternoon and told her he wouldn't be able to make it to the Lightship tonight because he had a touch of food poisoning. Claudine was kind and sympathetic. "It might be a virus. Get a good rest. I know a hungry violinist I can get for tonight. He can use the cash."

Feeling it would be unwise, food-poisoned as he was, to be seen by any regular member of the Lightship audience dining out comfortably, he went at six-thirty to the delicatessen on the corner and bought himself a roast beef sandwich on rye bread, a ripe peach and a slice of Brie. He was on his way up the stairs to his room when Mrs. Oliva called from the foot of the stairway, "Telephone call for you."

The public phone in the hall was placed within a curved metal shield to provide partial aural privacy. There were guests coming and going, but their chatter provided another kind of privacy.

Buggie said, "I wanted to get you before you left for work. When you finish up tonight, get your ass over to my place, we have things to talk about. Things to straighten out." Hard cold commanding voice.

In a reckless mood of triumph and euphoria, feeling that he was through, magnificently through, with Buggie, Cosmo said, "By the way, I got your message, about Ron McCallister. And now here's one from me. From this day forward, Buggie, you can go right straight to hell." He hung up.

Glowing with independence, he went to his room, drank a very short scotch, and ate his dinner. In the middle of consuming the peach and Brie he bethought himself, got up, and locked the door.

He would like to have seen Buggie's face after that slam-bang glorious sentence.

Or would he?

He had the better part of an hour to wait until he left for the Chantrey house. It gave him a little too much time to think how dangerous Buggie could be when aroused. He found himself listening for footsteps in the hall outside, watching to see if the doorknob was being quietly turned.

Remembering the successful note-leaving technique he had used in his last personal interview with May ("By the way, I left a letter in my room to be opened in the morning in case I hadn't returned by then"), he wrote, this time, an actual note. To it he attached Buggie's communication on the drinks list from Sub Rosa's. He tucked the note into the frame of the mildew-spotted mirror over the chest of drawers.

At twenty minutes of eight, to allow for the traffic at crawl-pace on Commercial Street at this hour, he went—finding himself looking over his shoulder every other second—to his car in the lot behind Mrs. Oliva's and drove off to his appointment.

The rain had started again when Mrs. Lockett went up the Berry Path, through the pines, and around the house to the back door. She selected the right key from the Chantrey ring and let herself in. It was ten minutes to eight.

There was a dim gray light in the kitchen, coming over the tops of the blue and white toile cafe curtains, but the house beyond was in darkness. All the long curtains in every room had been drawn for the summer to prevent sun-fading. Turning on a light here and there as she went, she proceeded down the broad central hall to the main, or Southern Plantation, front door. Cosmo would of course approach by the grandest entrance here.

She had no idea if he would be armed, carrying, that is, his switchblade knife; perhaps he always carried it. The first thing would be to put him off his guard, if he showed any sign of wariness, put him at ease.

She opened the door a foot so so: welcoming gesture. Don't be found directly inside the door. Something too pointed, too watchful about that stance.

At a minute or so before eight she saw through the partly open door his car come through the pines, on the driveway. The drive went around to the rear of the house, where there was a large separate garage. He must have followed it to its end, because it was a long two minutes before he came up onto the porch. He couldn't, could he, have been hiding his car back there? Why? Or was it just normal orderliness, put the car where cars belong at this kind of house.

Lou Alveiro, who used a different vehicle every day for his present task and was now driving a dusty pale blue pickup truck, turned the truck and went to the battered phone booth a few streets back. The door was missing but the phone worked.

"He spent an hour in his room and then came out and got in his car. He drove along Commercial Street and he's just turned up Knob Lane."

"Thanks," Buggie said. "I'll take over for tonight. You might as well get started on your Hyannisport run."

"Good evening, Cosmo." Her manner was pleasant, neither warm nor cool. She wore her raincoat; the house was chilly. The chill didn't reach Cosmo. He was as happy and excited as he had been in years.

She reached into her leather handbag. "I've brought a pad and pen, will you jot down notes as we go along?"

She'd need her hands, free, if . . .

Without further preliminaries, they started a tour of the main floor, Mrs. Lockett casting out suggestions as they went. "As you see, the dining room is very large, perhaps we could knock down a wall to make an ell-shape, see this little den just off it?"

We. Thrilling, settled-on syllable, thought Cosmo.

"Just put down a rough idea of measurements, you'll have a good eye for that." They turned into the immense living room with three triple bay windows. "A gathering room, a room for private parties, I think, not an informal sitting room like the one at the Lilacs. We might even be able to take on small exclusive conferences here for a week's booking . . . Now, I feel that the library"—another great high-ceilinged room they had just entered through folded back double doors—"would form the nucleus of one especially grand suite. The Colonial parlor just off it would make a lovely snug bedroom. Look at those Delft tiles around the fireplace."

She herself looked at the left-hand light beside the front door. You hardly noticed the missing pane. But just in case—

"Here and there we'll see things that need repairing. Mrs. Chantrey, although she's a wealthy woman, has a way of putting off spending small incidental sums."

The butler's pantry, as large as most people's kitchens. The kitchen itself, at least thirty by thirty feet, two refrigerators. "Relatively new, she bought them three or four years ago. They wouldn't have to be replaced. But of course you'd like to see to things in here, running the dining room would be in your hands, you'd want to plan counters, an extra stove or two, and so on."

Cosmo busily scribbled notes on his pad. It was all very

well, even necessary, to start off like this, Mrs. Lockett thought, but time was ticking on. However, the second floor would probably be a better place, one felt vulnerable in the reaches of this big echoing main floor.

She had considered, late in the afternoon, the idea of bringing along some kind of formal statement for him to sign with the gun held to his head: saying that he would go away and stay away and that would be the end of it. She saw very quickly the futility of this. He would agree, sign, and then make a turnabout in twenty-four hours. He could even make the scene public if he chose to. "Would you like to hear what my wife was up to, last night, at the Chantrey house?"

There was no way out.

One final feature of the main floor was the large romantic glass-domed conservatory opening off the living room. It had a neglected look at the moment, the tall palms in their pots turning brown along their frond edges, a little puddle of rain on the rose-and-gray-streaked marble floor where there was a leak in the glass high overhead.

The conservatory set Cosmo on fire. "My God, what a fabulous bar-lounge this would make. A white piano. Hanging baskets on brackets, fuchsia, fern, trailing ivy . . ." He stood very still, gazing with love around the room, his setting, his stage.

"Well, yes, perhaps, it's certainly a thought. Now for the second floor."

An oak stairway of heroic dimensions rose from the center hall. The green carpeting made a wide footstep-softening path up it but a great deal of well-waxed and polished oak was on display, on the stairs and risers and the heavily carved banisters. One side was flush with the wall of the dining room and the other free. They climbed the comfortably shallow solid steps to the second floor.

TWENTY-ONE

Buggie left his car three-quarters up Knob Lane, pulled off the road into head-high pin oaks and scrub pine, and in a minute or two was standing among the curtaining long branches of the Norway pines.

A faint glow of light showed here and there on the main floor, through drawn curtains. Now another glow went on somewhere upstairs.

He was familiar with the Chantrey house, at least parts of it. When he had started up in his side business seven years ago, Mrs. Chantrey's only son, Neil, had been one of his first customers.

With the rain and the low clouds, it was dark enough to leave the pines and begin a slow circling close to the house walls. There, in back, was Cosmo's car, parked in front of the garage.

In those early days he had no couriers; he was his own delivery man. He had always used the side door of the house. Neil at that time, used the parlor, stripped, as his studio, where occasionally he dashed off an oil or water-color vaguely planned for a large expensive book in the indefinite future, to be entitled "Pictorial Provincetown." Actually doing little or nothing with his days and nights except enjoying life and the Chantrey money.

Buggie had brought a wide choice of keys, but before he had to do any experimenting with them he saw the missing pane in the light to his right. He bent and looked through the opening. One lamp lit, on a corner table. The room was empty. He reached in his hand, turned the knob, and silently entered the house.

The library was beyond this room, wasn't it? He tried to recall what he knew of the house geography as he stood, listening, in the center of the parlor. Not a sound to be heard except the rain on the windows and those damned, mourning, swishing pine boughs in the wind.

Hand in the pocket of his loose denim jacket, hand resting on his small gun, he advanced into the library. Did he hear something now? Higher up and quite a distance away? He stood just inside the other door of the library, the one that opened into the hall, and listened again.

Voices, upstairs. Not just Cosmo's. A woman's too. Probably the voices came from the far end of the wide corridor that ran to the left at the top of the stairs, windows on one side, bedrooms off the other.

He emerged into the hall and went halfway up the steps, flattening himself against the wall side of the staircase.

Who in hell was the woman? Mrs. Chantrey? It didn't sound like Mrs. Chantrey's voice, which was high and fluttery. Now he could hear better what was being said. They were still out of sight, above.

". . . a look at the last bedroom in this wing. I know you've already seen four, but this is different, the master bedroom."

Was she—and now he thought he knew who she was—trying to sell Cosmo Mrs. Chantrey's house, acting for her? Or was this to be a joint venture on their part? His mind, racing to try to piece the bits of the Cosmo puzzle together, gave him a shadowy sort of conclusion.

An extension of the Lilacs, hidden here in the pines. A so-called drug rehabilitation center. Wonderful kind of business to get into if you had the money, and a spotless reputation like Mrs. Lockett's. The rich getting addicted

family members out of their sight and off their backs. The
supply of drugs genteelly continuing. A nurse and doctor
in residence to see things didn't get out of hand. A luxuri-
ous country inn, in which to indulge yourself in peace and
comfort. He knew of one such place not far away, Twistle
Island off Martha's Vineyard, where he'd heard waterfalls
of money were coming in.

Everything fitted nicely into this frame. The early-
hours rendezvous, through her window, with Mrs. Lockett. The cello case now doing a two-way run. Cosmo's
brief and wildly expensive occupation of the Winthrop
suite, another secret conference, probably. And, most of
all, his sudden declaration of independence: "From this
day forward, Buggie, you can go right straight to hell."
The answer to which whispered itself immediately and
with finality in Buggie's head, "Okay, Cosmo."

They were quite near the top of the stairs now but still
hidden by the angle of the corridor.

"I want you to look particularly at the master bathroom
in here. Mrs. Chantrey never uses it because she says the
mirror walls make her nervous, but it's absolutely Roman,
the floor is Connemara marble."

He would open the bathroom door and she would be
two feet behind him. She couldn't possibly miss.

Twice so far, in their tour, when she was behind him,
she had fingered, through the leather of her handbag,
Major Yardley's pistol. Twice, she had dropped her hand
away.

Was she able to do this, after all? Did she want to? Don't
think any more, let her right hand settle the matter and
answer the questions for her. "You just cock the pistol,
push this slide back and pull the trigger."

Buggie thought it was time to move; at any moment
they could be at the top of the stairs. He ran down, and
under and behind the stairway, where there was a hand-

some mahogany telephone cabinet with a cane door. He went into the cabinet, leaving the door an inch open.

"I think we might be able to buy most of the furniture except her really good antiques," Mrs. Lockett said. They were in the long, gracefully proportioned master bedroom. "That teak chest inlaid with mother-of-pearl, for instance—very attractive but I don't think all that valuable, it would be nice to keep that."

Cosmo was tiring of beds and chests, rugs and closets, which she seemed determined to examine throughout the house—God, how many rooms, how many floors, still to go?—no matter how long it took. He was lured by large, grand, sweeping plans but didn't care much for the nuts-and-bolts aspects.

His mental eye was downstairs, in the conservatory, which felt as if it had been especially created for him alone.

He went over to the teakwood chest and switched on the radio that stood on it. Before turning, he saw in the pier glass in the corner beyond it her hand groping in her handbag. She lifted her head, and their eyes met in the mirror. Something about her eyes terrified him obscurely.

Music was pouring radiantly through the room, Beethoven's Second Symphony. Her hand drew out from her bag a paper tissue. The tissue was shaking, so her hand must be too.

Taking her completely by surprise, Cosmo went swiftly toward the open hall door and not the bathroom door. "Excuse me for three minutes, May. I can't wait to try out the acoustics in the conservatory—don't be startled when you hear me roaring out 'The Volga Boat Song,' " and he was in the hall and starting to run eagerly down the stairs.

She collapsed onto the bed in a half-sitting position and found her face buried in her hands.

A thought pierced her near-fainting confusion. Was this, his flight, disaster?

Or, was it salvation.

Because she couldn't, again, summon up the will to . . .

Cosmo turned right at the foot of the stairs. The double doors of the living room were still folded back, the conservatory beckoning greenly beyond the opposite open doors.

Buggie, from the telephone cabinet, shot him through the back of the head, twice, when he had just entered the living room.

He heard the thud of the big body hitting the rug, and an unspeakable few sounds mumbled, gurgled, into the blind looming face of death. Then, silence.

Buggie momentarily considered cutting and running. Mrs. Lockett might very well be immobilized with terror, upstairs. The sound of the two shots seemed to crash and echo interminably through the great solid house, which as well as keeping outside sounds out held and remembered, in its depths, powerful sounds within.

But, too chancy. Already she had screamed, a thin scream, partly a wail. Only once.

He pulled the cane door closed. There was no light to speak of here in the cabinet under the stairs. Hung from a rail at the top of the door, inside, was a heavy brocade curtain that could be drawn for further privacy and soundproofing when the telephone caller wished no faintest syllable to be overheard. He pulled the curtain across the door, leaving only a narrow strip of cane to look out through.

A sound of footsteps, slow, on the stairs almost directly over his head.

Wait it out, sweat it out. See what happens. He had no other choice. And he had his gun.

Nothing could happen to him. But no point in something final and fatal happening to her. No point in complicating simplicities that had just been taken care of.

There wasn't a great deal of sweat about it after all. Mrs. Lockett reached the bottom of the stairs, then he first heard and now saw her crossing the bare parquet floor of the hall.

She stopped several feet outside the living room door and looked at what was on the floor inside. She made a little clicking sound in her throat. She said, just above a whisper, "Cosmo . . . ?"

Of course she wouldn't get an answer. Ever.

Thank Christ, no womanly fooling about with the body, pulse and heart and so on, Buggie thought. He could imagine very vividly what the back of Cosmo's head looked like.

She turned and ran. He heard the front door, on pneumatic springs, closing quietly and softly in response to the backward push of a hand.

She was still running when she reached the Berry Path. And crying, or gasping, both, frantically wanting air in her lungs.

She had done it, then. Shot him, killed him. Followed him downstairs when he was on his way to the conservatory. And then had blanked it all out, erased the unbearable, gone back upstairs and then allowed herself to scream, at the echo of the shots . . . ?

Yes.

No?

She paused under a dripping tree when she was almost home and felt in her bag for the pistol. She touched the nose of it. Cold. Wouldn't it be hot if it had been fired? Twice?

Don't, on this dangerous cliff-edge of a panic that might go plunging on its way into madness, don't think.

Hide this ruin, this Mrs. Lockett, in her apartment. Hide her fast before her desperate crying, or screaming, tore apart the rainy night.

If she was going to call the police, the nearest phone would be at the Lilacs. And she must have come here on foot, he had seen no other car but Cosmo's. That gave him at least five minutes, even if she ran. The police would take another, at least, four minutes to get here. That gave Buggie a total of nine minutes.

He ran down the lane to his car and was driving along Bradford Street in under seven minutes. And ten minutes after that, he was grilling hot dogs at the Caper.

TWENTY-TWO

On Saturday morning, while mowing the lawn at the Chantrey house, Aaron Vell noticed that the loose pane had now fallen in. Mrs. Lockett should have done something about it, but Lord knows she was busy enough at the Lilacs.

He stood looking at the square hole. Thief-inviting kind of opening, right near the knob. Maybe thieves had already accepted the invitation. Or squatters. Maybe he'd be held responsible by Mrs. Chantrey. It might be a wise thing to take a look inside.

Four minutes later, his face green under his weathered brown, he called the police. "Body here at Chantrey's, dead. Seems like he's been dead for days."

On Saturday afternoon, several sergeants went to check Cosmo's room at Mrs. Oliva's Bayview Lodge. The note in the mirror frame was the first thing that caught their eye. The note began, "In case of anything happening to me, I want it known that my life has been threatened by Buggie, otherwise George Eden. See attached warning from him on bar slip. As, it seems clear, he's already killed at least once, I feel it wise to take this precaution. Cosmo Fane."

Mrs. Lockett, whom Mrs. Captiva never remembered as being incapacitated by illness for more than a few hours or so in all their working life together, spent Thursday and Friday in bed. She informed Mrs. Captiva by telephone, in a raw hoarse voice, that she had caught a bad cold picking berries in the rain on Wednesday. "Foolish of me, but I wanted to beat the birds to them." She refused with thanks offers of attendance and hot soup. "I have everything here I want, I just need rest and quiet in bed." She also said no to Mrs. Captiva's suggestion of a doctor. "Much ado about nothing, just a heavy cold."

She was aware that certain physical symptoms could be psychologically produced, and all day Thursday ran a fever, varying from 100 to 102 degrees. Her bones ached, and chills coursed along her body under the blanket and the down comforter. It was helpful, at this time: you concentrated on your malaise, dragged yourself out of bed for hot tea, soup, and aspirin, and then crawled shivering back under the covers. She slept a good deal, which was also a help.

By Friday the back of her mind, which had never really stopped functioning, had worked things out, roughly, dimly.

She had not killed Cosmo and then drawn a merciful blank to wipe the killing away.

Someone else had been in the house. Someone else had shot Cosmo, dreadfully, in the back of the head.

She had no idea who. She had no idea why. The kind of life he lived, the risk-taking not very upright life . . . It could have been someone here in Provincetown, or someone who had tracked him from New York, or anywhere in the country.

She had every intention of dismissing the question from her mind forever.

The only circling, troubling thing, when she began to feel well enough to sit up in her chair late Friday afternoon, was a haunting fear that somehow, for some reason, the police might be calling on her. But why? No one could possibly connect her with Cosmo. For an awful sinking moment she thought, But I told Miss Winthrop's nieces that we were once married, and they'll tell the police. And then, clutching the arms of her chair, remembered that there were no Winthrop nieces.

Now, at this hour on Friday, there was still no explosion, not even a whisper, of the news of the murder at the Chantrey house, the body of Cosmo Fane found by . . . Who? When? Was he still lying there on the living room rug?

For the first time in her life while alone, she poured herself two inches of scotch and slowly, perseveringly, drank it all.

On Saturday she got up at ten o'clock, still feeling a heavy heart-thud whenever the phone rang. And it did, and often. Several friends wanting to know how she was, hadn't called sooner because Mrs. Captiva said she was in bed; didn't want to disturb her.

Dominic, saying, "Old Mrs. Carrots-and-Celery just checked out of the Winthrop suite, a New York banker and his wife want it for two weeks, all right? There's just one weekend booking in the middle of their two weeks and I'll put the weekend in the inn, or by that time the east cottage will be free, they may want that."

Beginning Thursday morning, she had been keeping her radio on, low, all day. The discovery of Cosmo's body by the Chantrey handyman, Aaron Vell, was the lead story on the Provincetown station's three o'clock news.

If the police did call, and ask her about her whereabouts on Wednesday night, why, she was here, of course, in her apartment. She had, on leaving to go out on her failed mission—which hadn't for some incredible reason failed —seen that the lights were on and the shades pulled to the sill. Vegetarian Mrs. Wicks, downstairs, was deaf.

Q2*

On the five o'clock news, the Cosmo story was repeated, with an addition: "Police have information that leads them to believe they have the probable identification of the killer, a local man."

A local *man.*

Mrs. Lockett, going to the kitchen in a haze, gave herself her second private whiskey in two days.

Another call, at six o'clock, Major Yardley. "Dear lady, and how are you this evening? Didn't call sooner because . . ."

"Much better, I'll be up and about and my old self from head to toe tomorrow."

"Bad business about that piano player, dead—and so near the Lilacs. I suppose you heard it on the news? Thank God I've got my trusty forty-five at the ready. In fact, I just cleaned and oiled it Tuesday. But on to cheerier matters. Suppose we have our long deferred birthday dinner tomorrow night, at the Lightship."

It wouldn't do to withdraw any longer, in any sense, from the everyday world. *Funny thing that Mrs. Lockett collapsed into her bed right after that man Fane was killed.* Not that anyone would ever say or think that. But common sense was common sense.

"What a nice idea, I'd love to. But could we make it Pepe's Wharf? The food there is so good, and the view of the bay so charming at night if we're lucky enough to have a window table."

"I'll call right now for our reservation, no ifs about a window table. See you tomorrow."

After dinner at Pepe's, over coffee and Key lime pie, Major Yardley proposed. He flushed and stammered a little and made somewhat of a hash of it, but a proposal of marriage it was.

Mrs. Lockett thanked him gracefully, and as gracefully and gently refused.

"I am afraid I'm a one-man woman, Major," she said. She looked out over the water. "After all these years, his death seems . . . only yesterday."

About the author

Mary McMullen, who comes from a family of mystery writers, was awarded the Mystery Writers of America's Best First Mystery Award for her book *Strangle Hold.* Her other books include *The Gift Horse, A Grave Without Flowers, Until Death Do Us Part,* and *Better Off Dead.*